Order this book online at www.trafford.com/07-2561
or email orders@trafford.com

Most Trafford titles are also available at major online book retailers.

Although based on historical characters and events, this book is a work of fiction.

Note for Librarians: A cataloguing record for this book is available from Library
and Archives Canada at www.collectionscanada.ca/amicus/index-e.html

Printed in Victoria, BC, Canada.

ISBN: 978-1-4251-5702-9

*We at Trafford believe that it is the responsibility of us all, as both individuals
and corporations, to make choices that are environmentally and socially sound.
You, in turn, are supporting this responsible conduct each time you purchase a
Trafford book, or make use of our publishing services. To find out how you are
helping, please visit www.trafford.com/responsiblepublishing.html*

*Our mission is to efficiently provide the world's finest, most comprehensive
book publishing service, enabling every author to experience success.
To find out how to publish your book, your way, and have it available
worldwide, visit us online at www.trafford.com/10510*

www.trafford.com

North America & international
toll-free: 1 888 232 4444 (USA & Canada)
phone: 250 383 6864 ♦ fax: 250 383 6804
email: info@trafford.com

The United Kingdom & Europe
phone: +44 (0)1865 722 113 ♦ local rate: 0845 230 9601
facsimile: +44 (0)1865 722 868 ♦ email: info.uk@trafford.com

10 9 8 7 6 5 4

ACKNOWLEDGEMENTS

Thanks to—Sara and Derek for their support and editing suggestions, and Lynda for her great enthusiasm. To Professor Thomas Acton of Greenwich University for his time and valuable critique. To Ilana Cork, Barnet Traveller Education Consultant, for patiently reading so many drafts, and Felicity Bonel from Greenwich Traveller Education Service for her encouragement. Thanks also to Jake Bowers from BBC Rokker Radio for the airplays.

The author wishes to acknowledge the generous support of GREENWICH TRAVELLER EDUCATION SERVICE for the production of this book.

SETTELA'S LAST ROAD

by Janna Eliot

Trafford
PUBLISHING

Settela, a Dutch Sinti Gypsy, was sent to Auschwitz. She was 9.

CONTENTS

Page

Chapter 1

Settela crouched behind a tree.

Her heart was beating so fast, she thought she was going to die.

Footsteps thundered along the river bank, coming nearer and nearer.

"Germans!" Kali whispered. "Keep still!"

Settela held her breath as the soldiers dashed past.

In the distance, someone yelled an order. There was a sharp crack and a cry of pain. Something heavy splashed into the river, and a wood pigeon squawked in alarm.

Settela froze, listening for the thud of boots. But the only sound she could hear was the drumming of her heart.

Slowly, she let the air leak from her mouth. Gripping Kali's arm, she stammered, "Who were they chasing?" Her voice was thin with fear.

Picking up one of the water buckets, Kali stepped from the shadow of the tree. "How should I know? Come on, they've gone now."

Cautiously, Settela left her hiding place and stood next to Kali in the sunlight. "What was that bang? Did they kill someone?"

"It was a branch breaking," Kali shrugged. "Stop your dumb questions! You're too young to understand! Get your pail! Mam's waiting for the water."

Settela followed her sister back to the safety of the encampment, her bucket thumping against her leg as she tried to keep up with Kali's long strides.

It's not fair, she thought. I'm old enough to carry heavy pails of water, but I'm not old enough to understand about the soldiers! I'm sure I heard a gun. I'm sure I heard a body fall into the river.

A breeze ruffled her hair, cooling her hot cheeks. "Perhaps the man swam away!" she panted.

"That's right, kid!" her sister agreed sarcastically. "That's what happened! Always give your stories happy endings!" Shaking her head and muttering a stream of curses, Kali turned off the track into the field.

"The best stories always have happy endings!" Settela shouted. "I know the man in the woods got away!"

Mam was sitting on the caravan steps, peeling potatoes.

"We saw some Germans, Mammie!" Settela called excitedly. "We had to hide! They were chasing someone!"

The potatoes rolled over the ground as Mam jumped off the step and snatched Settela's bucket, pouring the water into the washing tub. Messelo and Sonja ran up laughing, kicking potatoes across the grass.

"The soldiers won't bother us as long as we keep out of their way," Mam said. "We're quite safe—there's nothing to worry about!"

A half-peeled potato landed by Settela's foot. Bending to pick it up, she saw the fear in her mother's dark eyes.

Settela wanted to believe they were safe. But if there was nothing to worry about, why did Mam look so scared?

Chapter 2

Flames from the fire flickered and flared, casting frightening shadows into the night, but Settela knew her handsome father and older brothers would keep her safe. And Kali. No German soldiers or Dutch policemen would dare come near once Kali started cursing.

Settela was leaning against Mam's shoulder, pretending to be asleep. But she was listening for clues. She'd decided that if the grownups wouldn't explain what was going on, she'd just have to work things out for herself.

Sparks from burning twigs spat at the sky, swirling images into her half-closed eyes. Blood-red dragons. Silver horses. Orange butterflies.

Suddenly, Bacht neighed from the paddock and Lol barked a warning. Mam jolted upright, anxiously turning her head towards the road. Alarmed, Settela half rose, listening to the dull rumble of lorries and tanks on the highway.

"Nobody move!" Dada ordered. "Don't make a sound!"

Settela's scarlet fire dragons turned into monsters, the butterflies into ash. This is like a story, she thought, peering round at her silent family. It's as if everyone's been frozen.

The tanks lumbered onwards, past the little pasture, towards the north.

Dada sighed. "It's OK. We can relax. We're safe for now."

Removing his hat, he wiped his brow as everyone nervously settled closer to the fire. "That's decided it!" he said. "We *must* go to that special camp. We can't go on like this, jumping at every noise. We'll be safer there. The girls could have got shot down by the river this afternoon! And the soldiers might come for us at any minute. You have to be so careful. If you're in the wrong place at the wrong time..."

Old Django gave a warning cough and Dada lowered his voice, his words lost in the crackle of the fire.

So I *was* right, Settela thought. I *did* hear a shot in the woods.

Aunt Buta was talking softly to Mam about a friend called Esther.

"No one knows where she's been taken! Some say she's even been..." Her voice broke.

Settela leapt to her feet.

"Who's Esther, Auntie Buta? Who's taken her? Why?"

Kali gave her a warning look, but it was too late. Settela gasped as Mam's hands dug into her shoulders and shook her so roughly, the stars and moon seemed to fly round the sky.

"Girl, did I bring you up to question your elders?"

Settela tried to wriggle away. "Sorry, Mammie, but no one tells me anything! I only want to know what's going on!"

Dada threw more branches on the fire and picked up his violin.

"Let's have some music, forget about this damned war!" Smiling, he handed his bow to Settela. "Fix this for me, daughter, while I tune up."

Turning her back on Mam, Settela twisted the screw at the bottom of Dada's bow, watching the white horsehair tighten. She narrowed her eyes, imagining she was pulling her mother's long hair.

"Serve her right if all her hair falls out!" she muttered.

Picking up the golden lump of resin, she rubbed it over the hair of the bow. The resin glowed amber in the firelight, like a magic stone.

Elmo and Willy took up their violins, Dada nodded, and soon music was ringing out over the encampment. The tune took Settela back to the time before the Germans had come to Holland. To the time when she could pick berries in the forest without having to hide from soldiers. To the time when Mam was always kind.

Aunt Buta started to sing so sadly, Settela's eyes filled with tears. When the last notes of the song faded into the darkness, Old Django rolled himself a cigarette and cleared his throat.

"I've got a true story, just right for these difficult times. It goes like this."

Settela loved stories. She crouched on the ground next to little Sonja, listening to every word.

"In a small village not so far away, there lived a priest called Father Jacobs. He worked in the church, but he had a problem. A big problem. And his problem was this. He hated us Gypsies, us Sintis! He hated the way we travel around. Hated our freedom. Hated it when we went to his church."

Settela opened her mouth to ask why, but glanced at her mother and clamped her lips together.

"Now, one Sunday, Father Jacobs spoke out against the Sinti Gypsies. *Beggars and riffraff*, that's what he called us!"

Django mimicked the priest's posh voice, and everyone laughed.

"Well, Anna Maria, the doctor's wife, she was in church that day. She's a good friend to us Sintis."

"Yes, that's true," Mam agreed. "She's always helped us. She let us use her bathroom when we were camped in the little field near her house. The sink had taps with hot and cold water, and there was lavender soap in a little china dish. It smelled lovely."

Django spat out a shred of tobacco and went on.

"Anna Maria was that angry about the sermon, she jumped into her big black car and drove off to see the Bishop. And the Bishop soon put Old Father Jacobs straight. 'Our church is open to all,' he told him. 'Gypsies have as much right to pray as you and me! Priests and Gypsies are equal in the sight of The Lord!'"

Mam put her arms round Settela. "I know you're scared of the German soldiers, but Anna Maria will look out for us. She stood as your godmother, Settela. Held you when you were baptised, and you should have seen that Father Jacobs' face when he had to christen a little Sinti girl!"

Settela smiled at the familiar story and stared at the stars. Mam does love me after all, she thought.

Kali was sitting at the edge of the circle on a wooden box. Drumming her heels impatiently, she snapped, "Stop wasting time talking about rich Dutch folk! We should be planning how to get across the border! It won't be safe in that special camp they want to send us to! I'm going to run away!"

Dada waved his bow angrily, the horsehair silver in the moonlight. "You'll do what you're told, my girl! Where do you reckon you're going to run? You'd be caught as soon as you left the encampment! Holland's crawling with German soldiers and Dutch traitors—all looking for Gypsies and Jews! No! I've made up my mind. We're moving on tomorrow. To the special camp!"

Settela didn't care where they went, as long as it was somewhere she could run free and sing at the top of her voice. Somewhere without soldiers.

A cloud passed across the face of the moon, and the shadows lengthened. A cold wind rustled the leaves of the elms. Settela pulled her shawl round her shoulders, shivering as her father plucked a few notes, retuned a string and tucked the violin under his chin once more.

"Dance, little girls!" said Mam. "Dance while there's still time!"

The music poured into Settela's body, and she leapt up and started to spin around. She danced with Blieta and Sonja till her legs ached. When she danced with her sisters, she felt safe.

Even Kali joined in, moving her shoulders and arms in soft, graceful movements.

Chapter 3

Settela smoothed Bacht's thick mane, stroking his head while Elmo checked the horse's hooves. Inside the caravan, Mam and Kali were packing dishes and ornaments, wrapping them in cloth. Kali's voice could be heard through the open door, droning on and on, complaining about the move.

"Why doesn't Kali want to go to the special camp?" Settela asked her brother. "Moving on is exciting. We'll meet up with family and friends and have a big party."

Sighing, she patted Bacht's glossy neck. "Kali's never happy! She's always moaning about something!"

"We'll never get rid of that girl!" Elmo agreed. "Who'll want to marry her? She's a beauty all right, but she's got a tongue like a whip!"

Suddenly, Bacht jerked his head with a sharp whinny, and Settela stumbled back in fright. A large black car was chugging up the track, bumping over the muddy path. Quickly grabbing the reins, Elmo soothed the horse, pushing Settela behind him.

"Germans!" he yelled.

For a moment, everyone in the field stopped moving, and the pot Aunt Buta had been holding thudded to the ground with a hollow clang. The dogs chained beneath the wagons howled, straining to get free.

Willy rushed across the clearing to lift the younger children into the safety of the caravan, while the men snatched up sticks and shovels. Eyes blazing, Kali leapt down the wagon steps and picked up a big stone. With trembling fingers, Settela bent down for a pebble and stood next to her sister. She had to help save her family. She wouldn't let anyone hurt the little ones.

When the shiny car stopped on the narrow track, a beautiful lady in a red hat and a long red dress got out, carrying a bulging bag. The men lowered their weapons and waved to the stranger, and Kali dropped her stone. Smiling, Willy and Elmo walked over to the car, admiring the paintwork. Settela stared at the woman.

Mam peered out of the caravan door, Messelo and Sonja still hiding in her skirts. "Good Lord! I don't believe it!" she exclaimed. "It's Anna Maria Duysens, the doctor's wife! Whatever is she doing out here?"

Hurrying to greet the visitor, Mam called to Kali to fetch a clean cup. By the time Mam and Anna Maria had come up the track, Kali had poured a cup of tea and set an upturned bucket on the grass.

"Good morning, *mevrouw*!" Kali said in Dutch, covering the bucket with a clean cloth. "Please sit down!" She spoke so politely, Settela blinked in surprise.

The grand Dutch lady sat on the bucket, drinking tea.

"And how's the other Anna Maria?" she asked. "Come here, my dear, let me look at you."

Nobody moved. Settela glanced round, wondering who the other Anna Maria was.

Kali shoved her forward. "She means you, idiot! Have you forgotten your Dutch name's Anna Maria? That's the name on your Birth Certificate, you big clot!"

So this was the godmother Settela had heard so much about! She gazed at Anna Maria Duysens' pale skin and red dress. She put out her hand to run her fingers over the shiny crimson material, but Mam shook her head.

"This is the doctor's wife we were talking about last night," Dada explained. "The one who went to see the Bishop.

She held you at your christening, Settela, when Father Jacobs poured Holy Water over you."

The visitor took a book from her bag. On the cover there was a picture of a happy girl with golden curls and bright blue eyes.

"Anna Maria, my beautiful godchild. This is for you."

Settela had never held a book before. "Thank you, *mevrouw*," she said shyly, flicking through the pages. She looked at the illustrations and ran her finger over the black words.

"Don't she know none of us can read?" sneered Old Django. "Still, the paper will come in handy for starting a fire!" Settela looked at her godmother, frightened she'd be insulted by Django's comment. But Anna Maria was still smiling.

"Lucky for you she can't understand our language!" Kali snarled under her breath, glaring at Django.

Anna Maria stood up, taking Mam's hand. "My dearest Emilia! When I heard what was happening, I had to come to say goodbye. I can't tell you how bad I feel..."

She dabbed her eyes with a white hanky. Settela stared at the little red flowers embroidered round the edge, wondering why Anna Maria was crying.

"I expect she's worried about Auntie Buta's Esther," she whispered to Sonja. "That's why she's upset!"

Anna Maria took some loaves of bread, a pot of butter and a box of biscuits from her bag. "For the journey," she said, handing them to Mam.

Kali ran into the caravan, returning with some wooden tulips. "These are for you, *mevrouw*, to thank you for your kindness."

Beaming with pleasure, Anna Maria stroked Kali's hair, shook hands with Dada and Old Django, kissed Mam and Aunt Buta on the cheek, and hugged Sonja and Messelo.

Pulling Settela close she whispered, "Anna Maria. There's a special fire in your eyes, my dear. I will never forget you."

Dada glanced anxiously at the sky. "We'd best get going. We don't want any trouble. If we're picked up after dark..." His voice nervously trailed away.

Mam climbed into the caravan with the youngest children, and Willy got up beside Dada to help guide the horse.

Settela wanted to talk to her godmother. She wanted to sit next to her in the clearing and learn to read.

As Bacht clopped down the rutted track, Settela turned to wave to the doctor's wife, wondering when they'd meet again.

"Don't look back, child!" Mam said. "It's bad luck!"

Settela stared at the road ahead. She tried to bite down the question, but it jumped out of her mouth.

"Why's Anna Maria crying?"

She got ready for a slap, but her mother sighed and sat silently for a long time. "She's sad because of the war," Mam replied at last. "Her husband has to work for the Germans. And she's cross because we have to go away. Because the government says we must live in a special camp."

Settela wanted to ask about this special camp, but her mother closed her eyes. When a grownup did this, Settela knew it was best to keep quiet.

She'd ask Kali later, when they stopped.

Chapter 4

Settela was sitting outside the caravan in the new encampment, tearing a roll of green paper into strips. Kali miserably wrapped a piece of paper round a thin twig, attached it to a wooden tulip bud, and tossed the completed flower into a basket.

Kali glared at Settela. "Hurry up! We'll never get done at this rate!"

Settela ripped off another strip, and handed it to Kali. "I love making flowers," she said. "They look so pretty!"

Kali snorted impatiently, puffing out air between her teeth.

Wanting to make her sister smile, Settela tried to think of a question. Kali liked answering questions, it made her feel clever.

Settela looked round the camp, at the rows of caravans and the site office. "Why do they call this a *special camp?* What's so special about it? Why do we have to stay here? I don't like it. It's too big!"

Kali shrugged. "The only special thing is that now the soldiers and police know exactly where we are! And we're not allowed to leave! So they can come and pick us up any time they want!"

Kali sounded so angry, Settela wanted to run off to find her new friend Pipa. But she knew Mam would punish her if she didn't stay and help her sister, so she tore off another strip of paper and added it to the pile.

She thought of some more questions. "Why can't Pipa and Bettina talk Sintiska, like us? Why do they only speak Dutch?"

"They're not Gypsies, idiot brain! They're Gadje! Us Gypsies are clever, even little brats like you can speak Dutch and Sintiska. And some of our grownups know five or six languages. Because we move around. Because we like to travel."

"But Pipa's clever too!" Settela objected. "She can read. She's started reading Anna Maria's book to me. And Bettina, her Mam, makes great pancakes!"

Kali rolled her eyes. "Us Sintis, we don't need to read. Dada says only stupid people need to read and write! That's because they can't remember stuff like we can. Dada and Willy can play tunes without reading music. Even a daft kid like you can recite long stories off by heart!"

Settela wanted to argue, but she couldn't think of anything else to say.

Picking up the last oblong of paper, she tore it in two and stood up. An idea popped into her head. "If you're so clever, tell me why Pipa and her Mam have to live in this special camp! Like you said, they're not Gypsies."

Kali deftly wound the strip of paper round the remaining twig. "Those damned Germans don't like anyone who lives in a caravan!" she snapped. "So they've rounded up all the Limburg caravanners! Doesn't matter whether they're Sinti or Gadje. They've trapped us all!"

Mam came out of the caravan, a purple scarf over her hair. She was wearing large golden earrings and carrying a green satin shawl.

Mam draped the shawl round Settela's shoulders.

"Fetch the toys and pegs!" she commanded Kali. "Put on your pink blouse, and try not to upset anyone today! Just smile—we want the villagers to buy our stuff!"

23

Kali grunted and stomped off to get changed. Settela wriggled her shoulders, watching the satin cloth gleam as she moved. She danced about till Kali came back and kicked her.

"Why are you such a cow?" Settela yelled. "Why do you spoil everything?"

"You get on my nerves, that's why! Wait till you grow up, thickhead! Then you'll see there's nothing to be happy about!"

Mam swayed down the track with a basket of handmade toys and wild flowers, her headscarf fluttering in the breeze.

"You look beautiful, Mammie," Settela commented. "Wish I was old enough to wear a scarf."

"Fool!" Kali shoved her basket of pegs into Settela's hip. "You can't wear a scarf till you're married. And who's going to want to marry a skinny scarecrow like you?"

Settela stumbled and a wooden tulip fell out of her little basket. Laughing, she picked it up and stuck it behind her ear.

"Lemon face!" she sneered. "Bet I get married before you! Elmo reckons you're too grumpy to get a husband!"

"What makes you think I want to get married?" Kali screamed. "It's bad enough skivvying for everyone now, but at least I'm at home. Imagine having to live with a bad-tempered mother-in-law and being treated like a drudge!"

Settela frowned. She wasn't really sure if she wanted to get married either. She'd have to live with her husband in a new caravan, but she wanted to stay with Mam and Dada for ever. Still, it was no use getting upset about it. That's how things were and no one, not even Kali with her moods and tantrums, could change tradition.

Mam held up her hand in warning. "Stop arguing for a minute! Make sure there's no army trucks coming!"

Settela listened for tanks, but apart from a farmer driving a cart in the distance, the country road was empty.

She started humming a song about a lark flying in the sky, moving her feet in time to the music, almost dancing. She knew Kali couldn't stand it when she hummed.

Kali gave her a dirty look. "Walk properly, can't you?"

"Let the child dance!" Mam said. "While she can."

An odd glance passed between Mam and Kali, but Settela couldn't work out what it meant. She hummed louder, her voice tickling the back of her throat.

Before they went up the path of the first house, Settela examined the door. She could tell a lot from doors. If the door was red or yellow, with honeysuckle trained round the frame, it meant the people inside were kind and friendly. If a door was brown or grey, the person who opened it would be cross and rude.

This door was unpainted, with deep scratches in the wood, and a big iron knocker shaped like a skull. Horrible people live in this house, Settela thought. She wanted to warn her mother, but she knew Mam wouldn't listen.

As soon as Mam touched the skull, the door was thrown open by a small ugly woman.

"Good afternoon, *mevrouw*!" Mam began politely. Before she could say any more, the door slammed shut in her face.

"Bitch!" hissed Kali, spitting on the ground.

Mam turned and walked away, straight-backed like a queen. "Never show you're angry," she said as they went to the next house. "Always look proud!"

Sunlight shone on orange paintwork, and a lady in a yellow apron stood smiling in the doorway.

The woman patted Settela on the head. "Welcome, Gypsies! I need some pegs, and I'll take a doll for my little girl. Wait while I get the money."

When she disappeared into the house, the sound of barking came from an inner room. Kali scowled. "Probably going to loose her dog on us!"

Settela shrunk back. Sometimes when they went calling, people set dogs on them. Once, she'd nearly been bitten by an Alsatian.

The woman returned with a handful of money and a lump of bread and cheese. "I expect you've a lot of mouths to feed at home!" she sympathised, slipping the food into Mam's basket.

"Thank you, *mevrouw*," Mam replied, pressing a sprig of wild bluebells into the woman's hand. "Blessings on you for your kindness."

There was a sad atmosphere in the village, and the people they passed nodded dully.

"Most of their lads are away fighting the Germans," Mam commented. "That's why everyone's so miserable."

A woman in a shabby dress stopped them in the lane. "It's good to see you, Gypsies! You bring brightness in these dreadful times! My son's in the army, we've not heard from him for so long. Tell me my fortune, I beg you!"

The villager stuck out her hand and Mam took hold of the chapped fingers, turning the palm upwards.

"Your boy is well," she said in her deep fortune-telling voice. "He's a brave young man. He'll come back to you next winter."

A circle of women soon formed around Mam, and Settela walked through the crowd, selling flowers and pegs. She used the Dutch phrases her mother had taught her, adding a few ideas of her own.

"Who wants a pretty flower?" she chanted. "Lucky wooden tulips, made from lucky trees! They'll bring happiness to your home!"

An old man with a walking stick peered into her basket and chose two tulips. "One for my wife, one for my daughter—they're worried, you know. Our boy's off fighting at the front!" He blinked his watery eyes.

Settela wasn't quite sure what the front was, but she knew it was something to do with the war. She felt sorry for the tearful old man whose son was far away.

"Take an extra flower, *mijneer*," she said, giving him a red tulip. "Red's my favourite colour, it'll bring you joy!"

The man counted out coins with stiff fingers. "Thanks, little girl. Good fortune to you all!"

The village shop was stacked with packages and tins. Settela ran round the store, touching barrels, sniffing huge slabs of cheese. "Back behind the counter where I can see you!" ordered the shopkeeper.

"Thinks we're going to steal his rotten food!" scoffed Kali.

The shopkeeper didn't understand what she was saying, and Settela laughed, glad her family could speak a secret language. She stared at the red-faced man with the cross blue eyes.

It was almost dusk by the time they started walking home, their baskets heavy with food. Swinging her load onto her hip, Settela looked up for the magic evening star. The first star of the night was special, Aunt Buta always said. It made wishes come true.

There it was, bright as a newly scrubbed bucket in the dark blue sky. Settela closed her eyes, wishing for sweets or chocolate.

When she opened her eyes again, Mam was holding out a big paper bag. "Here, daughter. This is for selling all the flowers and dolls. Toffees to share with the other kids."

Settela popped a sweet into her mouth, offering the bag to Kali.

"Creep!" Kali snarled. "You won't catch me sucking up to old men and stupid women. And you, Mammie, you don't believe in all that fortune-telling garbage, so why do you do it?"

She closed her eyes, mocking Mam's palm reading voice. "Your son will return next winter. He will become a rich Captain and buy you a mansion in Amsterdam!"

Kali sounded just like Mam and Settela giggled. But Mam frowned, pointing at the cheese and eggs in her basket. "I tell them what they want to hear, it keeps them happy. Now we can feed our family. That's why I do it, my girl, so you can eat!"

Just then, the ground began to shake.

"Soldiers!" whispered Kali, pulling Settela beneath a hedge as Mam scrambled behind a tree. The rumbling grew louder and louder, and the earth trembled as two huge army trucks thundered by.

Settela pressed her hand to her mouth to stop herself screaming.

"Listen!" she whispered, as the noise died away. "I can hear people crying! We've got to get back to the camp! Something's wrong!"

The toffee in her mouth turned sour and stuck to her teeth.

Chapter 5

Settela chased after Mam and Kali, towards the shouts and screeches coming from the special camp.

As she got close enough to see, she stopped in horror. Her basket fell from her fingers. A bag of black-market sugar bounced on the ground, spilling over the muddy track.

Aunt Buta was standing by her caravan, screaming and pulling at her hair. Tikono was trying to comfort his mother, but each time he pulled himself up, he fell down again and wailed even louder. His sister Poscha was clinging to Aunt Buta's skirt, howling. Baby Doosje was squealing in Blieta's arms, and Messelo and Sonja were clutching each other, shaking with fright.

"What happened?" yelled Mam.

Aunt Buta sobbed so hard, Settela couldn't understand what she was saying.

"Find your father!" Mam commanded Kali. "He'll explain."

Aunt Buta tugged at her hair again. "No! Too late! He's gone! They took him! My Koleman too, and Rico."

Mam put her hands to her chest, gulping for breath. "Who's taken them? Where?"

"Police!" wept Aunt Buta. "Needed some Gypsies! That's what they said! Took 'em away! Dunno where!"

There was a low humming in Settela's ears, and a black cloud swallowed her. The camp was full of tears.

"What will we do without Dada?" she cried. She wanted to feel her father's arms around her, smell the tobacco smoke and resin on his jacket.

Kali's eyes flamed with fury. "We should have run away when I said!"

"Let's run now!" shouted Willy. "Hide in the woods!"

Bettina hurried up carrying a tureen of bean soup, followed by Pipa with Settela's muddy basket.

"Here, Emilia," Bettina said to Mam. "We're so sorry for your trouble. It isn't right. None of this is right. Eat this, keep strong for your kids. Tomorrow we'll find your men. I'll help you, I promise. We'll go to the police station in town."

"Charity!" sneered Kali. "I'm not eating their dirty muck!"

Glaring at Kali, Mam thanked Bettina, took the tureen and turned to her children. "Willy, build up the fire. Kali, fetch water. Settela, share out the bread. Sonja, get the mats..."

Soon they were sitting round the fire, forcing themselves to eat. Settela glanced at the sky, surprised the stars were still shining and the moon was so bright.

The sky should be grey and sad, like the feeling in my heart, she thought.

A heavy weight was pressing her down, it was hard to breathe. She looked round, hoping to see Dada tuning up his violin. But her father wasn't there.

"Tomorrow Bettina will help us," Mam said decisively, passing round pieces of flatbread. "She'll know what to do. She'll help me fill in forms and we'll get your Dada back, and Uncle Koleman and Uncle Rico too."

Settela stifled a sob. "I wish someone would tell us what's going on!" she mumbled to Kali. "Why have Dada and our uncles been taken away?"

Kali shook her head. "You'll get a smack if you ask the grownups any questions! You're too young to understand!"

Settela sighed. She knew children like her had to sit quietly and not disturb the adults, but sometimes it was too hard to obey the rules.

When the meal was finished, Old Django took Mam and Aunt Buta aside, talking to them for a while in a low voice. It seemed like Mam was arguing with him, but finally she shrugged and nodded. They sat back round the fire again, and Django cleared his throat and started to explain.

"Listen, little ones! We hoped that things would get better. We didn't want to upset you. But now it's time you knew the truth. Some really evil men from Germany have invaded Holland, Nazis who hate Gypsies and Jews."

A long lock of white hair fell over his face, and he poked it back under his hat and scratched his ear.

"The Nazis have hundreds of factories in Germany and Poland, so they need lots of workers. First they made the Dutch Jews help them, but now they need even more people. So they've started taking Dutch Gypsies."

Settela tried to imagine Dada working in a factory. She hoped he'd take care of his fingers. He needed supple fingers to play the violin.

"Yes," Django went on. "After what's happened here today, we must all be on guard." Hesitating a moment, he added, "I've a nasty feeling the Germans might come back again. For us all!"

A shiver ran down Settela's back. A little mouse scuttled out of the hedgerow, racing across the field, into the woods. As she watched it scurry away, she whispered, "What are these Nazis? Why do they hate Gypsies and Jews?"

Willy winked. "Don't be frightened, little sister. The Germans won't hurt us, they'll just make us work."

Is that true? thought Settela. If it is, why's Mam looking at Willy like that? Why's she pressing her hands to her chest? What'll happen to children who are too young to work, like Messelo and Sonja? Or me and Pipa? And what about old

31

people, like Django and Maira? And people like cousin Tikono, people who can't walk?

An owl swooped from the shadows. There was a squeal as a tiny field mouse was carried away.

Chapter 6

Lol started barking at dawn, his high angry yaps echoing over the encampment.

Settela stirred in alarm, but Kali just yawned and turned over.

"Probably scaring off a fox!" Blieta grunted sleepily, pulling the eiderdown over her head. Snuggling under the warm bedding, Settela closed her eyes again.

The caravan door splintered open.

She screamed as a policeman rushed towards her, shouting in Dutch, tearing off the quilt, dragging her from bed.

Yelling curses, Kali hit out, and Mam snatched up Doosje, hiding the baby in her shawl. Elmo and Willy jumped in front of the policeman and forced him to wait outside while the family dressed.

Shaking, Settela pulled on the first clothes she could find— a red blouse and a torn green skirt. She grabbed Messelo and Sonja, dressing them quickly.

She stood in front of her home with her frightened family, shivering in the cold dawn.

She couldn't believe her eyes. All the caravanners had been rounded up. Aunt Buta was crying, Django looked angry and ashamed, Bettina was as white as a sheet. Dogs snapped at the shouting policemen and were kicked away. Lol crept back to his place under the caravan, licking a bruised paw.

"What's going on?" people were asking each other. But nobody knew.

At last an officer gave an order. "Fetch your horses! Hitch up your caravans! We're taking you to another camp, a better one with more facilities. Hurry up now!"

"They're going to murder us!" shrieked Aunt Buta as Elmo and Willy ran to fetch Bacht. "They've slaughtered all the Jews, now they're starting on us!"

Settela felt the blood drain from her cheeks. Was she really going to be killed? That couldn't be true. There were so many things she wanted to do. She wanted to learn to read like Pipa, to go to France, to be a famous storyteller. She was too young to die.

"Stop talking rubbish, woman!" Django scolded Aunt Buta. "You'll frighten the children! You heard what that cop said. We're going to a better camp. When the war's over, we'll come back. You'll see!"

"That's right!" agreed Old Maira, the wise woman of the Sinti group. "Buta's exaggerating as usual!"

Settela stared round the field, trying to make sense of the chaos. She saw squads of uniformed men. Horses, snorting and rearing, were being backed into shafts. Little Dina and Fremdi were dashing about, trying to hide. Mothers were hauling their families into caravans, shutting the doors.

At last, walking alongside the wagons, the policemen led the way out of the special camp. "Anna Maria Duysens will come for us!" Mam promised her family, as Bacht pulled the caravan over the bumpy track. "She always helps us. She'll fetch the Bishop and they'll tell the police this is all a big mistake!"

Settela knew her godmother would come. Anna Maria, the doctor's wife, would sort things out. She'd make the Nazis set everyone free, and bring Dada home again.

There hadn't been time to make the usual preparations for moving on, and the dishes and ornaments rattled like tambourines as the wagon turned onto the road.

As the caravan lurched along, Mam and Blieta wrapped some of the china in old rags and Kali packed the objects into a sack, shaking her head and muttering furiously about traitorous Dutch policemen and cowardly German occupiers.

With a mixture of fear and excitement, Settela looked out of the window at the golden flowering gorse and the pink blossom of the cherry trees. Soon the countryside gave way to a town, where people were lining the roads to watch the huge convoy of caravans pass by. Some of the townsfolk turned away, others cheered, their children dancing after the procession.

I must work out what's happening, Settela thought. First there was that shot in the woods. Next we had to move to the special camp. Then they took Dada away. Now, they've come for us. Why? It doesn't make sense.

Willy pulled Bacht to a sudden halt, and Settela lost her balance, falling backwards onto Kali. "Get off me, you great lump!" Kali yelled.

"Where are we? Why've we stopped?" Settela yelled back.

With a thud, the door was flung open by a policeman.

"Everyone out! You'll need clothes and dishes! Bring your documents. And food for the journey!"

The caravan shook as Elmo scrabbled for the violins, Willy stuffed cheese and bread into a sack, Kali grabbed clothes and Blieta collected cups and plates.

Then the policeman started pushing them out of the caravan. "My book!" shouted Settela, wriggling from his grasp. "Anna Maria's book! I haven't finished it yet!"

The book, with the smiling child on the cover, lay amongst the clothes and broken pegs strewn on the floor. Settela just had time to pick it up before the policeman shoved her outside.

As soon as Settela's feet touched the ground, Kali snatched the book and stuffed it into a bag. "You stupid, stupid girl!" she yelled furiously. "That policeman could have killed you! All for some dumb book you can't even read!"

Settela flounced away from her sister. Tears blurred her eyes as she watched Django stagger from his caravan, his legs stiff with cramp. Tikono had fallen to the ground and was making rude gestures as he cursed the soldiers. Settela pressed her hand to her mouth, thinking the guards would beat him. But they just laughed as Willy ran to lift his cousin from the road.

A policeman loomed over her, threatening her with his fist. "Over there with the others!" he shouted. "Move your scrawny legs!"

Ducking to avoid the blow, Settela ran to her family, pressing her lips together to stop herself crying out.

"What's happening, Kali?" she whispered. "Are they going to shoot us?"

Her voice was trembling so much, she could hardly speak. Then Kali's arm was round her, squeezing her hard.

Baby Doosje began to wail and Mam took a piece of bread from her pocket, breaking off a tiny chunk. She held it to Doosje's lips, and the baby gnawed hungrily, gurgling with pleasure.

Mam handed out the rest of the bread. "Breakfast!" she said. She stood like a rock, her arms around her children.

Too scared to eat, Settela slipped the morsel of bread into her blouse for later.

Bettina and Pipa were nearby in the crowd, holding hands and looking terrified. Mam turned to Bettina and whispered something in her ear. Bettina nodded, taking a stub of pencil and a scrap of paper from her pocket. The pencil jerked over the paper as the policemen walked around, shouting and pushing people to the side of the road.

It must be nice to write, Settela thought, but what Dada said is true. Most people who can read and write are stupid. The policemen can read, but they're doing a really daft thing, waking us early in the morning and frightening the babies.

Putting her arms round Sonja and Messelo, she smiled at Pipa.

"I got the book," she told her friend. "We can finish it in the new camp."

Chapter 7

"We're at Eindhoven station," announced Bettina. "I came here once to meet my aunt from Maastricht."

Mam was staring hopefully into the distance, as if waiting for Dada to appear.

Settela touched her mother's arm. "Are we going on a train, Mammie?"

She hoped they were. She'd never been on a train. Once a little boy had waved to her from a train window, and she'd waved back from the caravan. That had been two summers ago, on the way to the pilgrimage in Zand.

An official hurried out of the station, trying to calm the unruly caravanners. "Be quiet! Stand in line! Stop running about! Get out your documents!"

Aunt Buta wept, but Mam's face was as still as a photograph. Settela watched the official strut around examining identification papers.

"That's Hans Stuypels!" muttered Old Maira. "Used to sweep the streets in Stein before the war. Look at him now—thinks he owns the ruddy place!"

Settela stood as close as she could to Mam while Hans Stuypels examined Bettina's documents. Moving on to Django, Stuypels frowned at the stained and crumpled papers, asking the old man questions. At last he stopped in front of Mam, blotting out the sun.

"Name?" he demanded rudely, staring into Mam's eyes.

"Steinbach, Emilia."

"Your papers!"

Mam rummaged in her sack. "I can't find our documents!"

"Hurry up, Gypsy! I haven't got all day!"

Mam lifted her head proudly. "We didn't have time to pack properly! Your men only gave us a few minutes to leave our homes! I don't know where our papers are! Stand away and let me look!"

He'll shoot her, Settela thought, clutching Mam's arm in fright. But Hans Stuypels flushed and stepped back.

At last Mam found the documents at the bottom of a sack, and when Stuypels had checked them, he turned to move on.

Elmo defiantly barred his way. "What about our animals?" he asked. "The horses and dogs? What'll happen to our caravans? You can't steal our property like this!"

The official handed over a sheet of paper. "Don't you worry, lad! All you caravanners will get your stuff back. I don't suppose you can read, but this here's a receipt. That's why we need your names, see? We've got records of your goods. Just keep this receipt safe, and hand it in to a police station after the war. You'll get what you deserve, you can be sure of that!"

Looking suspiciously at the receipt, Elmo folded it carefully and stuck it in his pocket.

As Stuypels moved off, Mam let out a shuddering sigh and put her arm round Settela. "We'll be alright!" she said.

Settela tried to smile.

"Into the station!" yelled the policemen, waving their guns.

Grabbing Messelo, Settela followed Mam onto the platform.

A huge shiny train was waiting on the tracks and Settela skipped towards it, dragging Messelo behind her.

"Look! We're going on that train! Now *we'll* be able to wave at children from the window!"

"Quick, get on, you caravan rats!" shouted the policemen, pushing the prisoners on board.

Grasping Sonja's hand, Mam clambered up the steps, calling to Settela to follow. But as her mother disappeared through the carriage door, Settela's excitement turned to fear. Something was telling her not to go on the train. Something was telling her to run.

She was looking round for somewhere to hide when Old Django bent down and took her hand. "Come on, child! You don't want to be left behind! You'd not last five minutes on your own!"

Putting his foot on the train steps, he tugged her aboard.

"So this is what it's like inside a train," Settela murmured. "A long corridor on wheels with lots of doors and windows!"

"In here, quick!" Kali called, pulling Settela through an opening.

"Oh!" Settela gasped. "It's lovely." She was in a narrow room with leather seats, wooden tables and curtains. She ran to the window and peeked out at the guards and caravanners on the platform.

Django settled himself into a seat and hunted in his pocket for his tobacco tin. He gave Elmo and Willy a stern look before offering it to them. "Surprised you two lads are still around! Some of the young men took off this morning when they heard the cops coming. They had the right idea!"

Elmo glared. "Have you forgotten they took our father away yesterday? We have to look after our mother and the children." He rolled himself a cigarette, his eyes sparking with anger.

"How will Dada know where we are?" Settela asked, trying not to cry. "How will he find us?"

"He'll go to Anna Maria and she'll tell him," Mam answered comfortingly.

Settela turned back to the window. The platform was empty now, apart from the stationmaster and a Dutch woman. The woman turned away, sadly shaking her head.

"Look, Sonja! That poor lady's crying!" Settela said. "Probably isn't enough room for her, so the guard won't let her on!"

The train puffed clouds of steam as it chugged out of the station.

Old Maira came hobbling into the compartment, escorted by a soldier. "Well, there's nothing we can do about it, so we'd best get on with it!" she said, grinning round. Crouching on the floor, she tucked her long skirt under her heels, making herself comfortable.

"So, we're on a train," she went on. "First time ever for most of us, right? Let's imagine we're going on holiday, like rich folks. We'll have a picnic. Look, here's a bit of cheese. Got anything else?"

She spread a clean scrap of cloth over the table, placing a curling slice of cheese on top. Mam added an apple, Aunt Buta cracked open a hardboiled egg, and Django pulled a flask of water from his back pocket.

Settela remembered the piece of bread in her blouse. Proudly, she put it on the cloth.

Kali stood up. "We need to wash our hands before we eat! There's a washroom along the corridor, but one of those guards is standing outside it."

Mam frowned. "Take Settela. Ask the guard if you can wash your face. He won't hurt you if you're with a little girl."

"Come on then, kid!" Kali said. Settela followed, proud she'd been chosen to help her older sister.

The train was swaying like a caravan in a storm, and she had to hold onto the walls to keep upright. The guard looked at her rudely, but when Kali smiled at him and shook her beautiful long black hair, he winked and stepped aside, opening the door.

Settela gasped. She was in a gleaming white washroom. There was a sink with taps. There was a bar of white soap. On the wall hung a wooden roller with a stiff linen towel. "This must be like Anna Maria's bathroom," she exclaimed, sniffing the soap.

She turned on the taps, laughing as water gushed out. Although it didn't smell of lavender, the soap was soft and creamy and she lathered it over her cheeks, splashing warm water over her face and hands, combing her wet fingers through her hair.

While she waited for Kali, she looked at herself in the silvery mirror. Thick black hair, smooth brown skin, dark eyes. When she smiled, her teeth sparkled. She put her left hand on her hip and turned her right shoulder outwards, like Mam and Aunt Buta did when they had their pictures taken.

"My mother has a young baby," Kali told the guard as they went out. "She needs to wash her."

Kali gave a dazzling grin, and the man shrugged. "Let her come. Let them all come. Makes no difference to me!"

Settela stared out of the window, a tiny slice of apple in one hand, a piece of cheese in the other. The train sped past windmills and farms, past canals where people were working on barges.

She saw tanks, and soldiers marching along the roads.

"Fascists!" Elmo spat out. "Invaders! It's because of them we've been chucked out of our homes!" He drew a menacing finger across his throat.

Flanked by motorcycles, the German army rumbled along. A soldier in the back of an open lorry looked up and waved as the train passed by.

"No! Not you!" Settela mouthed. "I *am* looking for someone to wave to, but I'm not going to wave to a German soldier! You're a Nazi and you hate Gypsies and Jews! No way am I waving to you!"

At last she saw him. A little boy sitting on the bank of a canal. Just as the train drew level with the tiny figure, a woman wheeling a pram came along and pulled the child up.

He twisted back to look at the train, waving his free hand to Settela. Settela waved and waved till the little boy was a spot on the horizon. A warm feeling spread through her. I've done it, she thought. I've waved from a train.

"Stop fidgeting!" snapped Kali. "Why can't you ever sit still?"

Old Maira begged some tobacco from Django and lit up her pipe, puffing contentedly as Aunt Buta started singing. Squeezing next to Mam, Settela rested her head on her mother's thin shoulder, humming along to the sad melody. Aunt Buta's voice rang out into the corridor and people in other compartments joined in.

If we sing loud enough, maybe Dada and my uncles will hear us, thought Settela.

The song floated out of the window.

Chapter 8

"Wake up, Settela! Get up!"

Slowly, Settela opened her eyes. The train had stopped. Willy and Elmo were collecting luggage from the rack, and the man who'd been guarding the washroom was now standing by the door of their compartment, looking stiff and cross.

"Where are we?" Kali asked the guard, but he didn't reply. Even when she smiled at him, he remained silent.

Old Django shuffled over to the window and peered out. "I recognise this place. Came to visit my cousins here when I was a lad. We're near the village of Westerbork."

He sounded puzzled. "Wonder what they've brought us here for! No factories in this area! This is farming country!"

"Get moving!" called the guard from the doorway, looking at Kali. "Come on, my beauty! Out!"

Settela knew the man was an enemy. So why was he helping Kali carry a heavy sack into the corridor?

Settela's feet seemed to stick to the carriage floor. "Don't get out!" she cried. "Something terrible's going to happen! Stay on the train! Hide under the seats!"

No one was listening. Kali grabbed the sack and hurried Settela onto the platform. There was nowhere to run, nowhere to hide.

"Hurry up! Form a line!" shouted soldiers as prisoners jostled to rejoin relatives and friends.

bbing, Aunt Buta heaved Tikono onto her back. "No
wling!" scolded Maira. "You'll only make things worse.
Stop your noise! Look after your kids!"

Settela glanced at Mam, expecting her to tell Maira to leave
Aunt Buta alone. But Mam didn't speak.

This is very weird, Settela thought, as they were hustled
out of the station. It's like being in one of Django's stories.
I guess someone will come to rescue us soon, a big bird or a
flying horse or the spirit of the woods. Or the wind will blow
us into the sky, and we'll hide in the stars.

She looked around for a magic figure, but could only see
guards and straggly rows of people. Tired hungry children and
frightened confused adults stumbled along the path with bags
and cases, whispering to each other.

"Look for a way to escape!" Elmo muttered. Settela nodded.
But the soldiers were always there, shouting and watching,
making sure no one moved out of line.

A bird circled high overhead in the late afternoon sun.
Pulling Messelo behind her, Settela trudged after her brothers
and sisters, trying to keep up. What if I get lost, she thought in
panic. What if Messelo and me are left behind, on our own.

The thudding of her heart made her dizzy.

"Halt!"

They had stopped in front of a long building. As Settela
tugged Messelo over the grass to stand by Mam, Aunt Buta
and Poscha began a high wailing. Children pulled away from
their parents, squawking like terrified birds.

The guards lifted their guns. "Stop that racket!"

"Mammie, they're going to shoot us!" Settela shuddered,
pressing her face into her mother's chest.

Mam's soothing fingers stroked her head. "It's all right,
my sweet!"

Then someone started speaking in a deep polite voice. "I
am Camp Commandant Albert Konrad Gemmeker. Please be
quiet. There is no need for alarm."

45

Settela looked up to see a tall man in a dark uniform towering over the crowd.

"If you will do what you are told, no harm will come," he said in Dutch. His strong German accent sounded so funny, Settela and Poscha giggled, holding their fingers over their mouths to stifle their laughter.

"First, you will wash, then a doctor will check. After, you will rest. We will give food."

The Camp Commandant saluted and walked away.

"Food!" said Poscha. "Chicken stew!"

"Mmmm. Fresh bread and potatoes," smiled Settela. The cousins grinned at each other, rubbing their stomachs.

A cold wind had started to blow, so Mam tucked Doosje under her shawl, while Settela squatted on the ground between Kali and Sonja, trying to keep warm.

"We'll wash in a nice bathroom, like on the train," Settela murmured to her sisters. "With lavender soap like Anna Maria's."

"I'm scared!" lisped Messelo. "Wanna go home! Don't like the nasty men."

Slowly, Settela turned her head in all directions. She had to find some place to hide. But there were too many soldiers pointing guns at the waiting prisoners.

"We'll go home soon," she promised, tickling Messelo under the chin.

"Come on, you vagabonds!" yelled a guard, beckoning to Mam and Aunt Buta. "We're going to clean you up! Women and girls first."

Prising her hand from Messelo's grasp, Settela followed her mother into the long building.

She was in a large whitewashed room. A harsh electric light beamed from the ceiling. A bittersweet smell pricked her nostrils.

Something wrapped itself around her foot. She looked down and screamed.

"A snake!" she shouted in horror. Mam was staring at the floor too, shocked.

Snakes were signs of bad luck.

"Stop yelling!" Kali snapped. "It's not a snake."

When she looked again, Settela realised that a long lock of thick black hair had caught around her ankle. I must be dreaming, she thought. I can't make sense of this.

But before she had time to work out why hair was lying on the floor, a man's voice thundered, "Take off your clothes!"

Settela turned to Mam, sick with disgust. Women never undressed in front of men. It was a sin. She stared from Mam to the men with rifles. She waited for Mam to explain to the guard, to smile and say that everything would be all right.

But Mam just stood there, clutching Doosje in her arms. The guard slowly lowered his gun and aimed it at the baby.

Mam's huge black eyes emptied of expression. Mam handed Doosje to Kali. Mam took off her shawl slowly, proudly, like a queen. Her slim fingers undid her blouse, one button after another.

Mam's overskirt slipped to the floor. Then her underskirt. The inner skirt.

Mam stood in her long petticoat.

"And the rest of your filthy gear!" the guard ordered. Mam stood still. The guard waved his gun at Settela.

Settela heard Aunt Buta moan and Doosje laugh. She saw the baby's chubby hands patting Kali's cheeks. She screwed up her eyes, waiting for the bullet, waiting for the pain.

But nothing happened.

Hours seemed to pass. Cautiously, she opened her eyes and glanced at her mother. Mam was staring into the distance.

At last Mam spoke in a low, flat voice. "Children, take off your clothes. Stare at the floor. Don't look at the men."

Settela, Kali and Blieta undressed the younger children and slipped out of their own clothes. Shivering, Settela draped her long hair over her body. There were goosebumps on her skin. She had never stood naked in public before, never in her whole life. It was the deepest shame.

Now she was being pushed towards a shower. Water poured over her, stinging water. Hands were rubbing her head and body.

"Leave me alone!" she heard Kali shout. There was a scuffle and her sister fell to the floor.

It was a nightmare. It couldn't be happening.

"Kali, be quiet!" Mam begged. "Just do as they say."

"Dada will be here soon," Settela wept. "He'll save us." Tears poured down her cheeks. Cold water sloshed over her head, taking her breath away.

Sometimes Dada told a story about a violinist who played such wild music, the wicked prince and his soldiers danced and danced till they fell down dead. Then all the Gypsy prisoners burst their chains and escaped to the mountains.

"Come to us, Dada!" she sobbed. "Play your violin. Play till the guards fall down dead. Come to us, Dada, and lead us to freedom!"

Chapter 9

The guards stood to attention, clicking their heels together like Hungarian dancers as the Camp Commandant entered the room. He sat down and gazed at the group of women, crossing his legs and smoothing a crease from his trousers.

Kali muttered a curse.

"Nobody move!" warned Mam. "Be still!"

Settela tried to keep still, but she was so cold and wet she started to shiver. When the Commandant barked out an order, Mam was pushed into the centre of the room where a woman in a white coat was sitting at a table.

Settela stared at the floor again. Someone threw a thin scratchy towel over her shoulders and she quickly dried herself, hiding her body with the rough material.

"Next!" said the man. Kali and Poscha, Aunt Buta and Sonja shuffled forward, one after the other. And still Settela stared at the floor.

At last a guard pulled her into the centre of the room to be examined.

The doctor's gentle fingers tapped her chest. A pen scratched on a pad. The doctor said something and the Commandant took a crisp white handkerchief from his pocket, holding it in front of his mouth.

The door opened and a woman in a striped dress with a star on the front came in, placing a pile of clothes on the table.

Amongst the neatly folded garments, Settela recognised the red blouse and torn green skirt she'd put on that morning.

She quickly shrugged on her clothes, tugging at her blouse. As she fastened the buttons, the smell from the blouse tickled her nose and she stared at the Camp Commandant in alarm, trying to stifle a sneeze. He was sure to shoot her if she made a loud noise.

With watering eyes, she remembered the trick Mam had taught her, and pressed her cold fingers round her wrist. The sneeze turned into a quiet cough which the Commandant didn't seem to hear. He continued calmly running his hands along the seam of his trousers, looking at the women before him.

Settela helped Sonja into her skirt. "We're still alive," she mumbled to her little sister. "Things aren't so bad now we're dressed."

Her stomach gave a low growl and she wondered when they were going to eat.

But it seemed there was another thing to be done first. The woman in the striped dress picked up a huge pair of silver scissors and beckoned to Mam.

"They're going to kill her!" Settela screamed in terror, and she threw herself forward, clawing at the woman. "Leave my mother alone!" she screeched. "Don't hurt her!"

The guard pushed her back to Kali, who gently took her hand. "What are they going to do to Mam?" Settela sobbed. "When are we going to escape?"

"Be patient, little one!" Kali replied hoarsely. "Mam will be OK!"

When Settela looked up, a strange woman was standing in front of her. A bald woman. A woman with Mam's face but enormous wild black eyes. A shiny skull. A ghost.

Settela shrieked.

Aunt Buta was dragged to the chair, holding her hands over her head, squealing like a rabbit in a trap. A few moments later she was released, her dark hair now carpeting the floor.

"Do me next!" commanded Kali, stepping forward. She sat down like a client in a village hairdressing salon, glaring proudly at the Commandant. Stunned, Settela watched Kali's beautiful thick hair fall to the floor like feathers from a plucked bird.

"No!" Settela screamed.

The guard pointed at her. "Now you!"

Biting and scratching, Settela was thrown into the chair. There was the flash of gleaming scissors. Steel blades slashed her glossy hair. A razor scraped her scalp. She stared ahead, choking back tears.

She was pushed back to Mam.

Mam hugged her and tried to speak. "Don't worry, daughter," she whispered at last. "It's just hair. It'll grow back."

Settela was silent. Her head felt cold and light. Mam always said the hair of Sinti women was their greatest treasure. They cared for their hair so carefully—only cutting the ends on the night of the new moon. They smoothed their hair with crushed herbs, they washed it in pure water from streams.

Shaving a woman's head was the punishment for the most terrible crimes, like murder or running off with someone else's husband.

"Namen?" yelled the soldier at the desk.

"Steinbach, Emilia." Mam's voice cracked like ice on a river.

Mam gave her official name. Tutela, her Sinti name, was secret, used only by family and friends. When the guard pointed at Settela, Mam said, "Anna Maria." Settela wanted to laugh, it sounded so funny, so Dutch. Then she started to weep.

She imagined Anna Maria Duysens, her godmother, in her long red dress, drinking coffee from a golden cup, while her husband, Doctor Duysens, ate salmon rolls and cream cakes from a silver plate.

Squeezing her eyes shut, she willed a message to the distant market town where her godmother lived. "Save us, my dear Anna Maria! Come and take us away!"

"I'm thirsty," whined Poscha, rubbing her head.

"Suck your tongue," Blieta advised. "Like this!" She demonstrated, making loud sucking noises.

The guard threatened her with his fist. "Shut up, Gypsy scum!"

At last the women were pushed out of the room. They stood on the open scrubland, blinking at each other in the spring evening.

Settela stared round at the shorn women, at the children with shiny scalps. Were these bald strangers really her sisters and cousins?

After a while, a group of old men came out of the building, cursing and shouting. Settela screwed up her eyes, trying to think where she'd seen them before.

"Mammie!" one of the men shouted. "What have they done to you?"

Mam looked vacantly at the man, touching her newly shaved head in disbelief. Her scarf hung loosely from one hand, the bright material fluttering in the breeze, like a flag. As if waking from a nightmare, she blinked, rubbed the scarf over her raw scalp, and tied her headcloth quickly in place.

"Elmo?"

Settela couldn't believe this hollow eyed youth was her handsome brother. Looking round for Messelo, she saw the little boy standing alone, opening and shutting his mouth like a fish pulled from a pond. There was a red mark on his head where the razor had scratched him.

When Settela hugged him, he trembled in her arms.

On the grass lay a pile of battered cases, sacks and boxes.

"They're all wet!" exclaimed Willy. "They smell funny, like our clothes."

"When?"

"Soon!"

In front of them, reaching to the horizon, stretched a huge purple heath. At the side of the path she could see large barns set behind barbed wire enclosures. Outside some barns stood groups of thin people wearing shabby clothes with stars on their sleeves. Settela stared at the stars. Golden stars. Beautiful. Gleaming in the twilight.

"When will we get our stars?" she asked.

"Stupid—they only give stars to Jews!" scoffed Kali.

Disappointed, Settela stared at the Jews as they passed. Some of them had dark eyes like her. But their eyes looked dead.

"Yaya!"

She glanced round to see who had made the sound.

Messelo pointed inside the compound. A small lad was lying in the dust by the barbed wire fence, wearing a threadbare jacket topped by a golden star.

"Starchild," said Settela in Dutch. "Hello!"

"Yaya!" laughed the boy. Messelo tried to wriggle under the wire but Settela pulled him away.

"Wanna play with him!" Messelo whined.

Settela yanked him back. "Keep walking! Do you want the guards to hit you?"

She forced Messelo along, trying to think. Why was the little starboy enclosed by wire? Why was her family being marched along this path? What were the Germans going to do to them?

Where could she run? Where could she hide? She looked around, searching for some way of escape. That's what Dada would expect her to do. One day, she'd be famous, and the Sinti people would sing songs about her. About Settela, the girl who led her people to freedom.

Lost in her dream, she bumped into Blieta as the line of prisoners halted outside one of the barns. "Watch it!" snapped her sister.

When the guard waved his gun, the caravanners began filing through the door. But Settela hung back. She couldn't go into this stinking black place. She would not go inside.

"What you waiting for, Gypsy girl? Into the barrack!" a voice ordered roughly. "No more sleeping under the stars for you! No more special camps! Time you lousy caravan trash learned how to sleep inside, like civilised folk! That's the orders!"

A shove sent her tumbling over the threshold. Peering through the shadows, she cried out in panic.

Her mother had disappeared.

"Mammie!" she screamed.

Her voice was lost in wails of darkness. She would never find her mother again.

She felt Messelo's arms digging into her, squeezing the breath from her body.

Then she heard Mam's voice. "Settela, Messelo, over here!"

The single light in the centre of the room threw dark shadows over the narrow bunk where Mam, Sonja and Blieta were huddled together.

Giddy with relief, Settela pushed Messelo through the long barn. Past weeping women and children. Past groups of men muttering angrily to each other.

"What are they going to do to us?" cried Aunt Buta, clutching Poscha and Tikono.

Mam gave a smile. "Everything will be alright."

"God will protect us!" said Maira.

Roza ran her hands over her scarf. "They'll soon let us go!"

Settela sensed the terror behind their brave words. Her legs shook and she felt sick. Then she heard Anna Maria's voice ring through her head. "Settela, my child. You have a special fire in you."

Straightening her back, she tied her scarf tighter, poking her finger into the uncomfortable fold of cloth beneath her chin. She would find a way out of this nightmare.

A faint breeze fanned her face and looking round, she realised it was blowing through a crack running down the side of the wall. Making her way through the room, she put her eye to the crack and peered out. In the deepening dusk she saw two figures entering the compound, carrying a heavy bucket between them.

"Grub's up!" shouted a guard from the doorway. "Get outside and help yourselves!"

By the time Mam had led her family into the compound, the guards had disappeared. Kali and Poscha collected brushwood and twigs, the men built a fire, and Blieta balanced a rusty pot of water in the flames.

The women looked inside the food pail.

"Rotten potatoes!" exclaimed Bettina. "Stale bread!"

"Carrots full of worms!" Aunt Buta groaned. "We can't give this to our children!"

"So what will you give them?" shouted Mam. "We can't be too fussy! Cut out the worst bits, boil the rest!"

"What do you want us to cut the potatoes with?" screamed Bluma. "You have a knife?"

"Use your teeth!"

"Wait!" said Elmo, opening his violin case. He fumbled in the little resin compartment and took out a penknife.

"Come on!" Settela said to Sonja. "Let's find something to make the food taste nice!"

Behind the barn, the guards were squatting on wooden boxes, smoking, looking up at the stars, their rifles dangling from their shoulders.

Sonja drew back. "They'll shoot us! I want to go back to Mam!"

The men were talking sadly in German.

"Don't be scared!" Settela soothed her frightened sister. "They won't bother us while they're smoking! Look, there's some nettles and wild mint over there."

They ran over to a gravelly mound where a few stubbly plants were growing. Wrapping a clump of long grass round her fingers, Settela tugged at the nettles, placing a handful in her skirt. Sonja picked the mint, burying her nose in the sweet leaves.

Settela gazed across the camp, counting the guards stationed round the open heath. A little to the left she saw a high tower where a soldier with binoculars was keeping watch.

As she led Sonja back to the fire, she imagined all the prisoners were following her across the heath to the shelter of the forest. They were singing a song about her, about Settela, their great heroine. About Settela, the little Sinti girl.

Spreading out her skirtful of nettles, she started to hum, dancing in time to the music.

Chapter 11

Willy and Elmo were standing by the barrier, prodding the wire with their shoes.

Mam chopped the mint and nettles, and stirred the herbs into the pot. The other women searched in sacks for cups and bowls, and served out the watery stew. "Lads, come and warm yourselves," Maira shouted. "Food's ready."

"We're looking for a gap in the fence!" Willy called back.

"Here, children, bread from the camp kitchen," said Aunt Buta, breaking the hard loaf into pieces.

Sonja quickly stuffed the grey lump into her mouth. "Yuk! It's horrible!" she complained, spitting it out. Settela chewed her bread. Sonja was right. It *was* horrible. It didn't taste like the flat soft bread Mam made back home. This bread was as hard as stone, and tasted of sawdust and grass. She dipped the crust into her soup and sucked.

Mam held her hands to the flames, a dreamy look in her eyes. "Dada will be here soon. He'll take us home and we'll eat rabbit and fried onions."

Licking her lips at the thought of her favourite meal, Settela carefully carried two cups of soup to her brothers and stood with them as they drank.

Moonlight glinted on the barbed wire fence, throwing lacy patterns onto the grass. Slipping her hand through the wire mesh, she asked, "When are we going to escape? Tonight?"

At Elmo's warning cough, Settela stopped talking and quickly pulled back her hand. Guards were marching into the compound, pushing everyone inside the barrack.

"In you go!" yelled the guards. "No dancing round fires for you Gypos tonight!"

Their enormous black shadows flickered on the ground, hideous giants waiting to eat her alive. "Come on, little one," Elmo said, taking her arm. "I promise we'll escape soon."

Settela lay on the hard bunk, squeezed between Kali and Blieta. Doosje was snuffling in Mam's arms, and Sonja and Messelo were babbling to each other. She heard Willy and Elmo working out escape plans on the upper bunk. Aunt Buta was weeping, Old Django was cursing. Maira was snoring. Tikono cried out in his sleep.

"I don't understand," Settela mumbled. "This must be a nightmare. It can't be real. Two nights ago we were happy. In our own caravan, in our special camp. We had food and water. Lovely long hair. We had Dada. Now we're in this stinking barn they call a barrack. On a hard plank. Locked in like birds in a cage. Prisoners!"

"Shut up!" Kali grumbled. "Go to sleep!"

Settela ran her hand over her head. It was cold and rough, with a sore patch where the razor had scraped her scalp. She tried not to cry, but stinging tears burnt the back of her throat.

At last, she fell asleep.

In her dream the moon was huge and golden. Meat frying, potatoes from the farm down the lane, payment for a day's harvesting. Wild garlic and sorrel, sweet berries with a splash of cream. Men playing violins round the fire. Women singing, children dancing. Bacht whinnying softly from the pasture. Laughter. A comfortable bed.

Breakfast was a square of hard sawdusty bread and a sip of brackish water. Settela sat with Sonja and Messelo in the compound, breaking the bread into crumbs to make it easier to swallow.

She looked up as a prisoner with a yellow star hobbled through the gate, carrying a heavy pail. Sighing, the woman lowered the bucket, straightened up and rubbed the small of her back. The guard shouted something in German and checked inside the pail.

The prisoner glanced around and winked at Settela.

Settela gasped with surprise and delight. She recognised the woman. It was Anna Maria, disguised as a Jewish prisoner. The doctor's wife had somehow got into the camp to set her godchild free.

Settela wanted to jump up and shout, but she knew she had to keep quiet. She winked back to show she'd understood. She waited for Anna Maria to give a signal, but her godmother simply kept on rubbing her back.

She's trying to fool the guards, Settela realised. She's waiting till they go off for a smoke. Then she'll tell us where to run.

Now Anna Maria was winking at Mam. Mam nodded and walked over to her, and Anna Maria slipped something into Mam's hand. She just had time to whisper a message to Mam before the guard strutted up, pushing her out of the compound again.

Settela raced excitedly over to Mam. "Anna Maria gave you a gun, didn't she, Mammie? We're going to shoot the guards and run away!"

"Enough of your stupid stories!" snapped Kali.

"But Anna Maria..."

"Shut up about your bloody godmother!" Kali screamed. "She's no use to you now!"

"Be quiet, both of you!" ordered Mam, opening her hand to reveal something square wrapped in shiny paper. "That woman's just told me her name. It's Hannah, not Anna Maria. She gave me this. Stole it from the kitchen where they cook for the guards."

"Chocolate!" cried Messelo, turning a somersault.

"We'll save it for tonight," Mam said. "All you children can have a bit before you go to bed."

Settela blinked. So the starwoman wasn't Anna Maria. So Mam didn't have a gun. So no one had come to rescue her. Not yet.

Dark shadows of disappointment fell over her, and she gulped in despair.

Mam tucked the slab of chocolate beneath her shawl, and Settela turned to Sonja. "Dada will come for us tonight. With a box of chocolates tied with red ribbon. Like the one he brought home from that posh Dutch wedding he played at last year."

Sonja pushed her little hand into Settela's, smiling at the memory.

"Listen to what that Hannah told me," Mam said. "We're in a place called Kamp Westerbork. It's an enormous camp for Gypsies and Jews, with a kitchen and a toyshop. And a farm. All the prisoners in the camp have to work."

"A toyshop!" Settela grinned, putting her arms round Sonja and Messelo. "We'll work in the toyshop. We'll make horses and dolls, and spinning tops."

"Can I make a train?" pleaded Messelo.

Willy snorted. "I'm not working for those murdering bastards! I'm running away!"

"We're all running away," Settela agreed. "But first we'll make some toys to take with us."

She loved toys. Once Dada had carved her a beautiful doll for Christmas—a wooden doll with long black hair and brown eyes, in a bright red dress and green shawl. And one spring, Mam had bought a spinning top from the fair. When it whirled round and round it made a humming sound.

The spinning top was back in the caravan, far away.

Heavy footsteps. More guards. Lots of them. Holding rifles. Stamping their boots.

A soldier shouted a command in German.

Settela didn't move. She didn't understand. When the man shouted again, Maira stepped forward to translate. The old woman looked so frightened, Settela's knees began to shake.

"All us Gypsies from the special camp, we've got to stay here. But the rest of you, those who aren't Gypsies, you can go home. The guard says you've got to get your stuff and line up by the gate."

A piercing laugh echoed round the compound. Bettina, her mouth wide open, was giggling hysterically. Pipa ran to Settela and put her arms round her. Settela hugged her friend tightly, her stomach tight with envy.

"I want to come with you!" she sobbed. "Don't leave me behind!"

Bettina wiped her eyes with her sleeve, and went up to Mam. "You were right, Emilia," she said hoarsely. "They're only keeping you Gypsies here." She pulled a scrap of paper from her pocket. "Here's the list I wrote down yesterday at the station. I'll do everything you asked. I'll find out about your caravan and your horse and dog. I'll get in touch with that doctor's wife you're always going on about. I'll let her know what's happened. And when they bring your husband back, I'll tell him where you are. Pipa and me, we'll light a candle for you every night. For all of you!"

She pushed her sack into Mam's hand. "There's a knife in here, a fork and a cup. And my warm shawl. God bless you, Emilia, you've been a good friend. I'll never forget how you cured my Pipa of the fever in the special camp."

"But we have nothing to give you..." Mam's voice broke.

"I've got something!" Settela burst out, dashing into the barrack to rummage in her sack. At last she found the book Anna Maria had given her. She stood for a moment, running her fingers over the picture of the smiling girl on the cover. Then she hurried back to the compound.

"Here, Pipa," she said, her throat aching with sadness. "Take this. Finish reading it, you can tell me the rest of the story when I come home!"

She watched Pipa leave, longing to go with her. Longing to be free.

"Why are you keeping us here?" Bluma screamed at the guards. "Let us go too!"

Aunt Buta wept, lifting her hands to tug at her hair. She cried even harder when she remembered she was bald.

"Quiet, or I'll shoot!" threatened a soldier, but the women and children were so overcome by sadness, their cries could be heard all over the camp. Some of the men wept too, dry painful sobs.

At last, through her burning howls, Settela heard another noise rise up in the distance. A faint, soft, beautiful sound. The sound of men and women singing.

"It's the Jews!" Roza exclaimed huskily. "They're singing to us, to share our grief."

The song swelled up, deep and full of promise. Wild and full of tears.

The music wrapped around Settela, like a satin shawl.

Chapter 12

Rain fell through the night and most of the morning, the cold drizzle dripping through the leaking roof. Messelo stood beneath a hole, catching drops of water on his tongue, while Settela let the rain trickle over her cheeks, drying her face with the end of her pillowcase scarf.

When it rained back home, they usually stayed inside the caravans and slept, or told stories and sang. They made wooden pegs and carved flowers and toys to sell in the village. There was always work to be done, polishing ornaments or mending clothes.

But here, in this camp, there was nothing to do. Settela waited in the damp dark barrack for the rain to stop. For someone to come. She waited for Dada. For Anna Maria Duysens in her black car.

The grey morning melted into a grey afternoon which merged into a grey evening. The prisoners ate some grey bread and drank thin tasteless grey soup.

Settela wondered if Pipa was eating pancakes with maple syrup in her caravan in the special camp, finishing the book. Drugged with boredom, she sat listlessly till Messelo tugged at her skirt and pointed to the back of the room. "Look, Settela! Bluma and Roza are fighting!"

In a daze, she followed her brother to the stove, crouching on the dirty floor next to Dina and Fremdi. They all stretched their hands to the faint warmth of the furnace, watching the two women scratch at each other.

"Bitch! Baldie!"

"Bag of lice!"

The insults grew louder, the slaps harder.

"Stop acting like Nazis!" Maira yelled. "You'll have the guards in here if you don't shut up!"

"Who you calling a Nazi, witch face?" screeched Bluma. Roza rushed at Maira, pulling off her headscarf and trampling on it.

Mam defended Maira, pushing Bluma and Roza away. "Where's your respect for this old lady?" she shouted. "Shame on you!"

Settela looked at her mother proudly. Mam was so brave. Mam would keep everyone safe till they got out of the camp.

Shrugging, Roza dusted off the headscarf and handed it back, and Maira grinned, showing a mouthful of gold teeth.

"Just like old times, eh girls? We had plenty of rows back in our encampment, but then we could pull each other's hair. Not much fun, is it, my sisters, if you can't yank out a good handful of fluff!"

Everyone laughed. They sat round the stove, talking about fights back then, back in the days when they were free.

Willy and Elmo had been sent to the kitchen block with the empty food pails. Now they came clattering back into the barrack with rain glistening on their scalps, their eyes sparkling with excitement.

"Mammie! Auntie Buta!" Willy cried. "Dada and our uncles are OK! A guard in the kitchen told us they're in a camp called Amersfoort. They're being sent to Eindhoven soon. To work in a factory."

A smile softened Mam's thin face. "Dada's safe! I knew everything would be alright. He'll send for us, we'll all be together again."

She hugged Aunt Buta. "I told you things would be fine. Our men will get good wages, working in a factory!"

Elmo leaned forward, lowering his voice. "Listen carefully. We found out something else. Every Tuesday, a train takes prisoners from this camp to the East. That's a good time to escape. On the way to the station. We can run to the forest and hide. Wait till some Gypsies find us. Or till the Russian or British soldiers come."

Settela nodded. They'd run away. Pick berries in the forest. Find a wild goat and drink its milk. Wander in the woods till the war was over and Holland was free once more.

The rain had stopped drumming on the roof, and they all went into the compound to light a fire. Everyone was smiling because Dada and Uncle Koleman and Rico were alive and safe. Willy tuned up his violin, Elmo beat a rhythm on a rusty bucket, and Settela pulled Sonja and Poscha round in a dance.

"Dada's coming to get us!" she chanted. "We're going home!"

The music floated through the misty moonlight, over the buildings, to the hazy edge of the camp.

"Thank you, my brothers and sisters," called a Jewish prisoner, wearily returning to his compound. "A beautiful tune. May God keep you!"

"May God bless us all, my friend!" Django shouted back.

Boots clattered on the stony path. Guns glinted. Ugly shouting soldiers pushed everyone into the barrack.

"Silence, Gypsies!" barked a guard. "Listen! Be ready to leave by noon tomorrow!"

"Why?" Kali demanded. "What's going on?"

Settela held her breath, waiting for the guard to aim his rifle at her sister, but he didn't react.

"You're young enough to be my son, dearie!" jeered Bluma. "Shall I change your nappy for you?"

"Look at his cheeks!" laughed Roza. "Smooth as an apple."

The women sniggered, calling out lewd comments in Sintiska.

The guard looked at them and shrugged. "I don't understand your gibberish! It's all the same to me what you say! Just make sure your stuff's packed by midday."

He went out, locking the door behind him.

Poscha was trembling. "Where are they sending us now?"

Aunt Buta choked with tears. "We'll find out in the morning, my sweet one. At least we know your father's alive!"

Through the high window, Settela caught a glimpse of stars.

"We're going on the Tuesday train," she muttered to Kali. "We're being sent somewhere better. Maybe we'll see Dada. Maybe we're going home."

An icy tremor snaked down her back. "What if we're going somewhere even worse! Are they going to kill us?"

She shook her head. That couldn't be true. No one would want to murder little boys and girls, old men and women, just because they lived in caravans. Just because they were Gypsies.

Kali ran her fingers down Settela's cheek. "Don't worry, little sister. We'll be fine!"

Why's Kali being nice to me? Settela wondered. Something's up.

Night in the barrack. Fetid air. Thin bodies on a hard bed. Moonlight through the crack in the wall, a necklace of gold.

Chapter 13

Soft morning sunshine beamed through the narrow window. Settela swung herself down from the bunk to help Sonja and Messelo get ready. The rest of her family were already up, packing their belongings, slackening the hair of the violin bows, putting the musical instruments into cases.

While they were eating a hurried breakfast, Hannah, the Jewish prisoner, was marched in from the camp kitchen with bread for the journey. Making sure no one was looking, she took a small bucket from beneath her skirt and handed it to Mam.

"You'll need this, Emilia," she muttered.

"What for?" asked Kali sarcastically. "Collecting eggs?"

Embarrassed, Hannah whispered something and Mam nodded coldly.

"Well? What's the bucket for?" demanded Kali.

"We're going on a train," Mam said, "a long journey, it seems. And ..." she hesitated. "We're not allowed to use the facilities."

Settela immediately understood. It was forbidden to talk openly about such private things. She stared at the bucket. She tried to keep quiet, but words poured out of her mouth.

"They hate us, they call us filthy! But *they* are filthy! We haven't got enough water so we can't wash properly. My clothes are dirty—but at home I was always clean. My hair was long and pretty, but they shaved it off! They give us mouldy bread to eat, but at home our bread was soft and fresh. I don't understand! Why are they doing this to us?"

No one shook her. No one shouted at her. No one told a story to explain what was happening. No one sang a song. No one answered. There was just silence, heavy as a pail of water.

She felt Mam's arms enclose her, gently rocking her from side to side.

And everyone began to cry.

Boots marching through the compound. Guards. An open barrack door. Shouts.

Settela stumbled into the fresh air and the sunlight. Blinking in the sudden brightness, she looked at the clouds in the light blue sky. Larks winged over the camp, swooping round and round in a wild dance.

"God's bird," Mam smiled. "A lucky sign."

Settela laughed. It was the first time for three days she'd been outside the compound, and as she danced down the path she kicked pebbles into the air, ignoring the shouting soldiers and Mam's warnings.

Messelo trotted after her, panting after a few steps. "Feel giddy!" he complained. "Can't run properly."

"I'm dizzy too," Settela replied. "It's because we haven't eaten much. You'll soon feel better."

Revived by the warm air, she sprang and twirled like a lamb in a field. The sun beamed through her scarf, soothing her sore head.

She only stopped skipping when a wail rose from the column of prisoners in front. Squinting, she saw a guard prodding an old man to make him walk faster.

"So the Jews are leaving too!" commented Kali. "We must all be travelling together."

The man's pitiful shouts reminded Settela of the screams from the special camp, the night Dada had been taken away.

She looked round as she walked, searching for a gap in the trees, a hole where she could hide.

There was an opening in the hedge behind the Jewish barrack, a hole just big enough for a child to slip through. Her heart thudded as she sidled closer to the wire.

The fence was guarded by a uniformed man.

Settela kept on walking.

She was going to escape.

But she had to run soon.

Before she got to the station.

Before she was put on the Tuesday train.

Armed guards with hard, suspicious eyes marched beside the prisoners. Soldiers were everywhere, counting people, ticking lists.

And then, Settela and her family were on a platform, surrounded by dogs, surrounded by Dutch policemen, surrounded by German soldiers.

Dogs strained at the leash, eyes popping out of their heads, their jaws damp and red. One of the animals reminded Settela of Lol, and she moved towards it.

Elmo tugged her away. "Those dogs are savage!" he warned. "They'll have your hand off if you don't watch out!"

A train was waiting on the tracks. It was so long it seemed to go on forever. Guards were standing in groups, talking, looking at their watches.

"Engine's broken!" announced Django. "We've got to wait for a replacement. The soldiers are getting nervous—scared we'll make a dash for it!"

"This is our chance to get away," Elmo muttered. Heart thudding like a wedding drum, Settela edged closer to him, ready to bolt.

A sea of golden stars glimmered further up the platform. The Jews were waiting for the train too, carrying cases as if they were going on holiday. Most of the women were crying.

"Don't know what they're bawling for!" scoffed Maira. "It's the same for all of us."

Tears were trickling down Maira's wrinkled cheeks. "You're crying too!" Settela pointed out.

"Bless me, child, so I am! Must have some grit in me eye!" The old woman wiped her face with her grubby scarf.

There was so much to look at, Settela didn't know where to turn. In one corner of the station, guards were disinfecting luggage, even musical instruments. Two prisoners were pushing a trolley laden with sausages and packs of margarine towards the back of the train. Settela stared hard at the sausages, willing a packet to fall off so she could share it with her family.

Elmo smacked his lips. "Remember the smell of sausages fried with mushrooms? Wonder when we'll taste good food again!"

Stamping and swearing, Willy came back from the disinfecting area with the violins. "Damned idiots, ruining our precious instruments with their stinking water! Do they think our music's dirty?"

"Lucky they can't understand you!" Elmo hissed, wiping his violin with a rag. "Keep your voice down or you'll get a kicking!"

Settela dried Dada's violin case with her skirt. Dada always said their music was full of stars and sun and sky. And the clean wind which rushed from shore to shore. Before the war, the Gadje had come from far and wide to hear him play. Even Germans had driven across the border. They hadn't thought his music was dirty then. Before the war.

A woman's shout. A screech.

A stargirl was running along the platform, followed by a guard. The child's mother, screaming frantically, was being held back by a man.

The child stopped in front of Settela, grinning widely. Her pale blue eyes were very close together, slanting upwards in her wide face. Pushing her fingers into Settela's hand, she made strange gurgling noises.

Surprised, Settela looked at the little girl, at the star on her arm. She put her fingers to the golden cloth and the child giggled. The guard wrenched the child away, dragging her over to her mother. Before he handed her back, he slapped the little girl hard.

Settela cried out, but the child just laughed and rubbed her face. "Bang!" she giggled. "Bang, bang!" Roaring with laughter, she hit her other cheek. "Bang, bang, bang!"

The iron railway tracks started to hum, and peering into the distance, Settela saw pearl-grey wisps of steam whirling into the sky.

"Stand next to me!" commanded Kali. "Keep your eyes down, don't look at anyone. The guards are getting angry. Look what they did to that little kid! Anyone can see she's not right in the head, but that devil's turd still belted her one! May he burn in Hell!"

For a few seconds, Settela stared obediently at the ground. But as the noise grew louder and grey smoke swirled round her feet, she lifted her head. The engine shunted in like a huge metal dragon, spewing sparks and ash from greedy jaws.

Now there was even more to look at. Guards started shoving people into lines and a helper went by, anxiously wheeling an old woman on a stretcher.

"Look, Tikono!" Settela said to her cousin. "See that stretcher—it's made from cartwheels nailed to a plank of wood. Like the wheelchair Uncle Koleman made for you in the special camp."

The children stared as the stretcher passed by. At the end of the plank, near the old woman's feet, a case wobbled as the wheels rolled unsteadily over the platform.

"I'd like to know what she's got in that case!" Tikono said.

"Gold necklaces and earrings, I expect," Settela answered. "Books and gingerbread and lemonade."

When the helper turned the stretcher round, the case almost fell off, then the invalid was wheeled out of sight.

Messelo pointed at a tall man in jodhpurs and giggled. "Funny trousers. Looks like a penguin!"

Blieta pinched him. "Be quiet! That's the Camp Commandant. If he catches you laughing at him, he'll give you a whipping!"

Messelo turned to Settela, eyes full of tears.

Glaring at her older sister, Settela took the little boy's hand. "I won't let anyone hurt you!"

At last the guards started to push the prisoners aboard. The Jews were forced into the passenger compartments at the front of the train, staring out of the windows with ghostlike eyes.

The little girl who'd been slapped was still laughing. She waved at Settela and banged her hand on her cheek. Settela waved back.

Now another group of Jews in caps and overalls was marched along the platform, stamping their wooden clogs as they walked. "Death to Fascism! Long Live Free Holland!" one of them yelled, defiantly lifting a clenched fist into the air.

A soldier hit him round the ear, and the prisoner's cap fell to the ground, exposing his bruised, shaven head. Settela watched in horror as the man was thrown into a wooden wagon. There were no windows in the wagon, and the doors didn't close like ordinary doors. They slid shut and were bolted from the outside with heavy iron bars.

"Those men are from a camp in Brabant," explained Django, who seemed to know everything. "They tried to escape, so now they're being sent to Poland."

"I couldn't bear to go in one of those wagons!" Settela gasped. "There aren't any windows, you can't see out."

There was a roaring in her ears and she started to shake. Blieta patted her hand. "Don't panic, girl! We'll be OK! The wagons are only for prisoners who try to escape! We'll have a comfortable compartment, like the one we came in."

A scuffle and a shout. Settela squeezed to the front of the crowd to see what was happening.

One of the Jews was running over the tracks. For a moment everyone stared at the thin figure fleeing across the rails.

Then Branko, Bluma's nephew, was on the rails too, running for his life. It looked as if he was trying to chase the Jew. The golden star and Branko's worn soles flashed in the sun.

"Yosef!" a voice screamed in anguish. "Run, my boy! Run!"

"Branko!" yelled Bluma. "Get to Sweden, to Uncle Kundo!"

This was the chance Settela had been waiting for. She had to escape now. Taking a deep breath, she clenched her fists, ready to sprint to the woods.

A shot. A howl. A silence. A body on the line. Guards kicking something into the ditch.

"Don't look!" Mam's voice was shaking. "One of them got away, but I don't know who."

Settela's heart stopped beating. She felt sick. One of the men was dead. Shot. In front of her. And she didn't know who.

She'd known Branko all her life. He used to help Dada carry wood from the field, break ice on the river in winter. He knew where to buy the best horses, and how to train them. She prayed he'd got away. And that other man, Yosef. Although she didn't know him, she wanted him to live too.

There was a scream at the back of her throat, but Elmo was beside her, pressing her arm so hard she couldn't breathe. "Little sister," he murmured. "Be strong. We *will* get over this."

A dark mist clouded her eyes. "If I'd have run away, they'd have shot me too! I'd be dead!"

She shook her head, shocked that her life had nearly come to an end.

Her words were lost in the steam of the engine.

Chapter 14

The wooden wagon loomed over her like a deathly mountain.

"I can't go inside!" she gasped. "I won't be able to breathe!"

"It won't be too bad," Mam promised. "You'll be alright."

Maira was the first to be hoisted into the dark mouth of the wagon. As the blackness swallowed the old woman, her tattered bag burst open, the contents bouncing down onto the platform. A carrot, some bread, a battered cup, a bright hand sewn purse, a cracked clay pipe and a faded photograph.

A soldier laughed and kicked the carrot away. Silently, Kali retrieved Maira's possessions and strode up the ramp into the wagon. Turning at the door, she fixed her black eyes on the soldier with a silent curse, before disappearing from sight.

Red-faced with shame, the soldier heaved Mam on board and Willy passed Doosje and Sonja up into the shadows. Elmo picked up a sack and took Settela's hand, pulling her into the black hole. She tried to hang back, but Elmo's strong fingers clamped firmly round her wrist.

The murky wagon smelt of animals and manure, like Farmer Bruin's barn. Mam was sitting in the corner with Doosje and Sonja on her lap. Willy squeezed next to Mam, cradling the damp violins. Fumbling her way through the gloom, Settela squashed in between Blieta and Kali. Sweat dripped down her body, her heart thumped. The air, heavy and sticky, wrapped round her like a stifling shroud.

Shouts and thuds from further down the train made her jump. "What's that? Are they killing someone again?" The image of the body on the tracks shot into her mind.

"They're only closing doors, stupid!" snapped Kali. "Sliding bolts into locks."

Settela focussed on the shaft of sunlight shining through the doorway. Something was pulling her towards the brightness, and she struggled to her feet.

"Stop kicking me!" Kali yelled. "Why can't you sit down like everyone else?"

"I can't breathe," Settela groaned. "I've got to look at the sky!"

Stumbling over seated figures, she stood at last at the opening of the door, the air cooling her face, a breeze stirring the ends of her scarf. The Camp Commandant was walking along the platform, staring straight ahead, a little fat dog trotting by his side.

"Settela, watch out, or your head'll get stuck when they close the doors!" called Mam. "Come back over here!"

"Coming, Mammie!" Settela answered, but she didn't move. She could hear a commotion at the back of the station, where guards, yelling angrily in German, were dragging a man along the platform.

Settela ducked aside as the body was flung inside the wagon. There was a thwack and a squeak, and Tikono yelled, "Get off, you're squashing me!" When the man shouted back, Settela smiled with relief. It was Branko. He was alive. She tried not to think about the other man, Yosef, lying in a lonely ditch, with no one to pray over his body.

"Caught me at the trees," Branko was saying, his words slurred. "Knocked out some of me teeth, damn it! But I nearly made it! I almost got away!"

There was a grinding noise in her ear, like the sound of knives being sharpened, and Settela turned back to the opening. A thin man with a star on his arm was standing on the platform below her, tugging at the sliding door. Terrified, she stared down into his dull eyes.

"No, no, don't close the door! Let me out!"

Her words drowned in a screech of wood and metal.

Daylight was slowly fading from the wagon.

"When will I see the sky again?" she whimpered. "When will I breathe fresh air?"

"Settela! Come here at once!" Mam shrieked. "Before your head gets knocked off!"

She had one last chance to look out. To look past the man with dead eyes. To look at the Camp Commandant and his little brown dog.

And then she saw, to the right of the platform, something she'd not noticed before.

A man was hunched over a camera, pointing it directly at her face. Fascinated, she gazed at the photographer, at the glass lens glinting in the sun.

"Mammie!" she shouted. "A man's taking my photo!"

"Don't talk rubbish!" yelled Kali. "Get your skinny rump over here before I come and drag you back!"

The door closed with a dull thump. With a whine and a scrape, a bolt screeched into place.

Darkness. Screams. A child's high voice.

"Mammie!" She tripped over someone's feet. A hand struck her face and she scrambled up again. "Willy! Elmo! Kali!"

At last someone grabbed her. She recognised Kali's touch and sank down.

Her scarf had fallen off. She rubbed her prickly, itchy scalp, glad no one could see her bald head.

Then Kali started twisting and squirming, and pushed something into Settela's hand. It was a soft piece of material, torn from her clothing.

"Thanks," Settela whispered, knotting the rag round her head.

She slept in the airless wagon, dreaming of flames and dragons, witches and fire.

Hunger. Cramp. A train thundering onwards.

"O my God, save us!" someone shouted, over and over again. "What will become of us, dear Lord?"

Settela prayed too. "Sweet Jesus, stop the train! Lead us to the forests to be free, as we will be free in Heaven!"

The journey seemed to go on for ever. Sometimes the train stopped, but no one came to open the doors. Then it started again, on and on and on.

A shuddering floor. Foul air. A burning throat. A hard crust of bread. A sip of water. A bucket. Stinking, stinking darkness.

Chapter 15

Dada was scraping the wood of his bow across the strings, over and over and over again. Dada was calling her, warning her.

The screams of the violin turned into the screeching of brakes as the train slowed down and stopped. A crack of light split the darkness of the wagon as the doors grated open.

Dada was standing in the doorway, smiling at her, speaking to her. But he wasn't talking in Sintiska. He spoke in German. *"Raus, raus, schnell, schnell!"*

Dizzily, Settela staggered off the train, blinded by sunshine, tears of disappointment streaming down her face.

"Kali, Messelo, Willy, Elmo..." Mam called, assembling her children. She ran her fingers over their faces, checking they were all right.

"We're tired, thirsty, and very dirty," Mam croaked. "But we're together. We'll be fine."

Mam's voice is shaking, thought Settela. We're not fine. And we're not all together. Dada's not here. Uncle Koleman and Uncle Rico aren't here.

Soldiers stood on the platform, rifles poised to shoot. But not one of the prisoners tried to escape. They were too weak, too hungry from their three day journey.

"Where are we?" Maira mumbled, trembling with exhaustion.

"Poland!" Django answered.

As Settela gulped lungfuls of air, her head slowly cleared and she looked around. In the middle of the platform, she saw a doctor in a white coat sitting at a table.

The Jews, swaying in untidy rows, were being pushed forward one by one.

Settela rubbed her eyes. Was this another dream? Was a doctor really sitting on a railway station?

After a while she realised what the doctor was doing. He was sorting people into lines. One line was for old people and little children, another line was for young men and women.

As the prisoners hobbled to the doctor's desk, she tried to guess which line they'd have to stand in.

When all the Jews had been examined, the Sinti group was marched forward. "We're going to play the line game now," Settela explained to Messelo. He stared at her, his eyes dull from the dreadful journey.

"Mammie!" The scream was out of her mouth before she could stop it. "What if they put us in different lines? What if I'm left alone, without you? What'll happen then? How will I find you again?"

Mam didn't turn round. She followed Aunt Buta, cradling Doosje in her shawl.

"Stop crying!" Blieta ordered Settela. "Stay close to me and you'll be fine!"

To Settela's relief, the Sintis weren't examined by the doctor, but were loaded onto lorries instead. "What've you got to grin about, moron?" Kali scoffed, but Settela couldn't stop smiling. She threw her arms round Kali, who gave her a reluctant hug.

As they jolted along, Settela peeped out of the lorry, telling Mam what she could see. "Barbed wire. Barracks. Scrubland. It's a bit like our other camp, but much bigger. There's a high chimney with lots of smoke. It's so tall it stabs the sky!"

The truck stopped outside a low bunker. "*Raus!*" shouted the guards, banging the sides of the lorry with their rifles.

I'll slide off the lorry, Settela thought, and run out of the camp and hide in the forest. After that I'll dig a tunnel and rescue my family.

Willy lifted her down, his lips pressed together like an ugly scar.

Smoke crept down the back of her throat, making her cough, and she dabbed her watering eyes with her sleeve. Aunt Buta and Blieta clasped their chests, as if they were about to choke.

"You'll soon get used to the stink," remarked a guard. "We're only burning our dirty rubbish!"

The other soldiers laughed, and Kali looked at them with a mixture of scorn and terror.

"We'll be alright," Settela said, patting Kali's arm as they slowly filed into the bunker.

The first thing she saw was a prisoner in a striped uniform sitting at a table, some blue ink in front of him.

Settela smiled. "See that ink?" she said to Sonja. "The Germans want us to paint wooden flowers. To sell in the camp. I'm good at selling. I'll be able to buy extra food and tobacco for everyone!"

"And sweeties for me?"

"Sure!"

Someone called names from a list.

"Emilia Steinbach."

Mam was pushed into a chair and the man at the table took her hand, his fingers white on her brown skin.

"What's he doing?" asked Sonja. "Is he going to tell Mammie's fortune?

Settela frowned at the sight of Mam being touched by a stranger. "I don't think so!" she muttered. "You know only women can tell fortunes, so it can't be that."

The man soaked a piece of cottonwool in some liquid, and rubbed it over Mam's wrist.

Mam didn't move.

The prisoner dipped a needle into the ink, and stuck it into Mam's arm.

Settela screamed.

Mam's mouth was clenched, the veins stood out on her temples.

"Good!" the prisoner said, releasing her.

"What have they done, Mammie?" whispered Blieta.

Mam looked at her arm, at the blue marks etched into the swollen skin.

She turned to the man. "Don't hurt my children, my babies!" she begged. "You can't do that to them!"

The prisoner pulled up his sleeve to show a mark on his own wrist. "*Gnädige Frau*, I have to do everyone," he explained sadly. "We must all have a number. It is necessary for the camp records."

Aunt Buta's lips were trembling. "Does it hurt?"

"It stings, but you can bear it. You can all bear it!" Mam replied harshly.

Kali flounced into the chair and stared at the wall. She didn't move or speak, and when the branding was finished, she rose gracefully and walked proudly back to Mam.

Aunt Buta shrieked and pleaded, but her arm was marked with blue. —

I must get out of here before they do it to me, Settela thought. But suddenly she was in the chair, the man's cold fingers on her hand.

"Dada!" she wailed. "Why are they doing this? Why are they sticking a needle in my arm? Why do they want to mark me? Why are they hurting me so much?"

It was like the stinging of bees, like a snakebite, like the burning of nettles.

It was over.

She stared at the blue marks, wondering what they meant.

Sonja's voice seemed to come from far away. "No, no! Mammie, help me!"

Poscha groaned.

But one after the other, they were all tattooed.

Later, when the swelling had gone down, Settela tried to rub the ugly mark from her sore skin.

But it didn't come off.

Chapter 16

Another barrack, longer and colder than the first. Sleeping planks, a stove. High windows. Yearning eyes staring from thin unknown faces.

A woman stood up. Her voice was rough and it was hard to understand what she was saying.

"She's one of the Polish Gypsies," Maira whispered. "They speak a bit different to us Sintis."

"I'm Ezta, the Block Elder," the woman scowled, pointing to some empty bunks. "You lot can sleep in them beds. Been empty since the others died. Typhus they calls it. You gets it from lice and dirty water. There's a wash bucket on the table—water's filthy, but at least it's wet! Got any food?"

The newcomers were silent, their eyes fixed on the Block Elder. Settela twisted round, looking up at the sky through the narrow window.

"Don't think about escaping," Ezta warned. "Last week Marko ran off. We all had to wait in the Roll Call area in the pouring rain, while those Fascist bastards stood there barking questions all day long."

When Ezta coughed, a rattling sound came from her chest. "Fetched him back in the evening, they did! By that time, some of our women was more dead than alive, legs swollen like tree trunks from standing in one place for so long! And the kiddies were soaked through and starving. My little one's not spoken since!"

She pointed to a skinny child in rags, crouched in the corner.

"What happened to Marko?" Maira asked shakily.

"Dead! Strung up! And if they hadn't caught him, they'd have chosen ten prisoners, any ten, and shot 'em. As a warning!"

Settela shrank back. Ezta was leaning towards her, hands outstretched, sharp fingers digging into Settela's shoulders. Her foul breath scorched Settela's face.

She squirmed as Ezta stared deep into her eyes. "Think you can run away, girl, lead us to safety? Don't kid yourself! I see Death in your face!"

Pushing Ezta away, Mam wrapped Settela in her arms.

"You see Death in the mirror!" Mam shouted. "Take no notice, child! The woman's mad!"

Settela shivered and rubbed her wrist, expecting to drop down in a lifeless heap. But nothing happened.

Kali gave a deep sigh. "What is this place?"

Ezta cackled, showing blackened teeth. "Us Gypsies calls it Hell! Welcome to Hell!"

She laughed again. "Them Nazis have another name for it. They calls it Auschwitz!"

It was boring in the camp. Hunger, dirt, disease. Quarrels and fights. But the worst thing was the boredom. Every day the same. Get up. Stand in the sun or rain to answer your name at Roll Call. Hard bread with cockroaches in it. Rancid water. Sit around the barrack. Wait for someone from the kitchen block to bring food and news. Evening. Another Roll Call. Rotten potatoes or turnips. Sometimes a bit of mouldy meat. Nightmares. Week after week after week.

The chimneys loomed upwards, gushing smoke into the sky. The shadow of something foul and rotting hung over the camp, shrouding the barracks in an ashen haze.

Settela was so tired. She sat outside with Kali and the other children, remembering summer fairs with merry-go-rounds and stalls.

"It was so lovely," she said dreamily. "Dada played the violin in the evenings and all the Gadje danced. Waltzes he played, and polkas. Uncle Yanko gave me rides on the Big Wheel."

Messelo sucked his fingers. "Tell us about the candyfloss again."

Settela closed her eyes, thinking of the brook behind the Limburg pasture. Of juicy apples from Farmer Bruin's orchards, of cherries and pears and fried chicken. Remembering the taste of creamy milk. And biting into a chunk of yellow cheese. The memories were so vivid she could smell the cocoa. Pink candyfloss tickled her nose.

"I'll take you away," she promised Messelo and Sonja. "We'll go somewhere with clean air. A place without soldiers."

"Can we come too?" begged little Dina and Fremdi.

"Of course! I'll take you all to a country where people dance and play music. Where we can pick berries and bathe in pure water. Where we can travel freely in caravans. To the land where candyfloss grows on trees."

Just then, a harsh cry of pain rang out from the barrack and Settela leapt up in fright. Mam was standing in the doorway, holding a sheet and some rags.

"Kali, Settela!" Mam called. "Keep the young kids out of the way. Lalla's giving birth. Twins!"

Settela knew all about having babies. First the pregnant woman had to go into a barn or lie under a caravan. Then she screamed and cussed a bit. After a while there was the thin sound of a baby crying. The other women would wash the new mother, and help her into a soft clean bed. Later, after a rest, the mother would cuddle her tiny child. Her eyes would be dark and sleepy, and she'd look beautiful, like the Virgin Mary. Like the picture in the corner of the caravan.

Settela grinned. If Lalla was having a baby, that meant Anna Maria would come. Anna Maria had visited Mam the day of Settela's birth. Dada had tramped through the snow to the big house on the Market Place, to tell the doctor's wife about the tiny girl who'd just been born in the little pasture. About Settela, the Christmas baby. That's when Anna Maria had agreed to be her godmother. She could be godmother to Lalla's babies too.

Kali clapped her hands. "OK, kids! Sit on the grass while Settela tells a story! She tells good stories."

Settela was so surprised at Kali's praise, she couldn't think of anything to say. But then she remembered one of Maira's old tales.

"Once upon a time," she began.

There were screams from the barrack and the children leaned closer to listen to her.

"Once upon a time, a poor Gypsy from Eindhoven gave birth to twins, a girl and a boy. But in the morning, the girl was missing. Someone had stolen her, sold her to a rich farmer. Although the girl's Sinti name was Sonja, the farmer's wife called her Anna."

Contentedly sucking her thumb, Sonja smiled and wriggled closer to Settela.

"Anna grew up clever and beautiful, but there was a sickness inside her. She always felt lonely—she had a pain in her heart. Her parents took her to all the best doctors, but no one could ever find out what was wrong."

"Probably had lice!" said Dina.

"Or rotten food to eat, like us!" suggested Messelo.

"No, stupid, she lived on a farm!" Fremdi interrupted. "She'd have eaten radishes, and mutton, and apples."

"On Anna's thirteenth birthday," Settela continued, "some Gypsy musicians camped by the river, and the farmer and his family went to the village square to hear them play."

Settela stopped talking. Two newcomers had entered the compound, a stout officer in a smart uniform, and a prisoner in a white coat. The prisoner was carrying neatly folded sheets over his arm.

She watched as they walked into the barrack. Men weren't allowed to go near women in labour. She turned to Kali in horror, but her sister only shook her head in disgust and shrugged.

"Go on!" Dina urged. "What happened next?"

With an effort, Settela went on with the story.

"Like I said, the musicians were playing; an old man on the accordion, and a young lad on a violin. As soon as she heard the music, Anna's feet started to tickle and she began to dance. She danced so well, the Gypsies clapped. Then a woman came up and led her to the fiddler.

"The fiddler looked just like Anna, with the same oval face and the same dark eyes.

The boy stared. 'Are you my sister, the one who was lost?'

The woman hugged the girl.

'You are my Sonja, the one who was stolen.'"

The screaming from inside the barrack faded away, then Lalla started wailing again. Settela took a deep breath and continued.

"The rich farmer and his wife sat round the fire with the Gypsies.

'We didn't know she was stolen!' said the farmer's wife. 'A man said he'd found her in the church. He knew we longed for children, so we paid him what he asked. We cared for her as if she was our own.'"

Fremdi fidgeted impatiently. "What happened next?"

"They let the girl choose where she wanted to live," Settela explained. "And this is what she decided. 'I'll stay on the farm with the people I love,' she said. 'But I want to know my Gypsy family too. So, once a year, in summer, if you camp by

90

the river, I'll come to you and learn your language and your ways.'"

Settela finished the story quickly so she could find out what was happening to Lalla.

"Everyone agreed, and they had a big party with chocolates and pancakes and sausages."

Leaving the younger children arguing about their favourite food, Settela crept over to the barrack and peered round the door.

The officer was standing next to Lalla's bunk. "I'll look after your babies," he was saying. "I'll make sure they are warm. How can you keep twins in a place like this?"

"No! Don't take them!" Lalla's desperate screech pierced Settela's head.

"Do you want them to starve, sister?" cried Ezta. "You can't feed them! You have no milk! Give them a chance!"

The newborn twins squeaked like puppies as they were wrapped in the clean linen. Settela felt sorry for Lalla, but Ezta was right. Babies needed milk and warm clothes. The doctor would look after them, and give them back when they were older. They'd live with their mother in the summer, like in the story.

Then she saw Ezta's face. The Block Elder's green eyes were full of awful sorrow.

Settela sensed something terrible was going to happen to the twins, but she didn't know what.

The women spent the afternoon caring for Lalla. "She's so weak she'll die soon anyway!" Maira muttered. Mam and Ezta poked bits of bread into Lalla's mouth, gave her water, wiped her swollen face with rags.

"Where are my children?" Lalla moaned through the night.

In the morning, Lalla's bunk was empty.

"Where's Lalla?" asked Settela. "Has she gone to her babies?"

Mam's voice broke. "Yes, sweet child, they're all together now."

Settela smiled. The good news softened the dry breakfast bread, and she hummed her favourite tune.

Chapter 17

There was a red stain on Settela's bread, the colour of blackberry juice.

"Blood!" Kali told her.

"Blood?" echoed Settela. Running her tongue over her teeth, she tasted something metallic and sour.

"My gums are bleeding too," Kali said. "So are Mam's. It's because of the crap food!"

Kali spoke so quietly, Settela could hardly hear her. Once her brave sister would have shouted at the guards to bring fresh fruit and milk. But long weeks of imprisonment had dulled her eyes, changing her into a thin weak stranger.

The summer sun beat down on the iron roof, making the crowded barrack unbearably hot.

Settela lay on the bunk. She couldn't sit up. Something was crawling over her leg but she didn't have the strength to scratch. Her mouth throbbed. She wondered if anyone would ever come to save her. She wondered if anybody cared.

"Wake up!" Kali screamed in her ear. "The guards are taking us somewhere!"

"Settela, wake up!" sobbed Messelo.

Rough hands hauled her from the bunk, carrying her out of the barrack. She seemed to be on a lorry, jolting along a track. She felt Dada's fingers smooth her hair. He was taking her home.

"This must be the camp hospital," she heard a voice say.

There was a white room and sour smelling soap and a squirt of powder.

"It's antiseptic, gets rid of lice," the doctor explained kindly.

Mam smoothed her skirt down angrily. "We never had lice before. Only here, in this filthy Nazi place, have we got lice!"

"Shut your trap!" warned the guard, shaking his fist.

Settela started to sob, tears pouring down her cheeks. Even when the guard walked menacingly towards her, she couldn't stop crying.

Quickly, the doctor put his finger on her pulse, his brown eyes warm and sympathetic. "This child is suffering from nervous hysteria," he told the guard. "She needs food and rest."

Settela burst out laughing. She laughed and she cried. Grownups were so funny. They always gave things important names. They called big caravan sites *special camps*. They called barns *barracks*. They said tattoos were *identification marks*. They thought she had *nervous hysteria*. She didn't have nervous hysteria. She was just tired and very hungry.

She clung to her mother, shaking uncontrollably. Mam's sharp hip jutted into Settela's side, making her laugh even louder.

"I'll give the young girl some pills," the doctor said. The guard slouched back to his corner, lighting a cigarette, wafting tobacco fumes round the room.

"Dada's smell!" Settela murmured. "The smoke!" She longed to nestle into her father's strong arms and let his moustache tickle her cheek.

The doctor unlocked a drawer, shook some tablets from a bottle, and handed them to Mam.

"One a day, for the nerves," he said. "Start the treatment as soon as you get back to your block."

The guard stubbed out his cigarette, put on his cap and picked up his gun.

"We're done here! Shift yourselves!"

Later, back in the barrack, Mam opened the twist of paper the doctor had given her.

"Sweets!" she exclaimed. "Enough for all you children."

Settela sat between Messelo and Sonja, sucking her sugary treat. She wanted the sweet to last till the end of time. The sweet was a summer fair, a soft bed, a caravan, a blazing fire. It was a dance and a song and a father and the smell of spring.

She held the last morsel of sweet on her tongue, willing it not to melt.

At last it slipped down her throat, leaving a warm taste in her mouth.

Chapter 18

There was something different about the morning. A sharpness, a nervousness. Everyone felt it, but no one knew what it was.

So Settela wasn't surprised when a guard marched into the barrack holding a list. She'd been waiting for something strange to happen ever since the dreary day had begun.

"Step forward if I call your name. Some of you lucky people are off to work in Germany."

The prisoners listened tensely.

As the names were read out, Mam stiffened. Kali gave a start. Elmo looked at Willy and softly cursed. When Settela realised what was happening, the strength drained from her body and she slumped on a bunk.

All the prisoners stepping forward were aged between fourteen and twenty. The same age group as Kali and Blieta. The same age group as Willy and Elmo.

Settela squeezed her eyelids together. Hours seemed to pass. No Steinbachs were called.

The room was so quiet that when the guard rustled his list, the sound thundered through her ears.

The guard turned over a page.

"Elisabeth Steinbach, Johanna Steinbach, Willem-Hendrik Steinbach, Celestinus Steinbach."

"No!" yelled Settela, recognising the Dutch names.

Blieta burst into tears. Willy and Elmo embraced Mam. Kali calmly picked up her sack and grabbed Blieta's arm.

"Stop snivelling! Don't let them see you care! We'll go where they send us, do a bit of work. We're used to hard work. We'll meet up again when this infernal war is over!"

Bending over Settela she whispered, "Look after Mam! Take care of the little ones, my sweet darling sister."

Kali looked old and ugly, her eyes glittering feverishly in her yellow face. Settela clung to her, she couldn't bear to let her go.

"Don't leave me!" she screamed. "You've always looked out for me. Stay here! Don't let them take you away!"

She followed her brothers and sisters out into the compound, her heart aching as they were led off. The prisoners who were left behind wailed and lamented for their departing relatives, raising their hands helplessly to the cloudy sky.

"Go with God, my children!" Mam called.

"Willy, Elmo, be lucky!" shouted Settela. "Kali, Blieta, come back soon!"

As Kali's thin figure faded from view, Settela hurled herself to the ground. "Everyone I love is taken from me! My Dada, Uncle Koleman, Uncle Rico, Pipa. Our horse Bacht, our dog Lol. And now they've taken my brothers and my sisters!"

All around her, women were beating their heads on the earth, tugging at their clumps of hair. Most wept quietly, but here and there, a screech rang out like a string snapping on a violin.

"Heaven preserve my daughter!"

"Dear Lord, how could you let this happen to my boy?"

Settela wished for the world to end, for her pain and agony to be over. She prayed for Anna Maria to come.

"Have you forgotten us?" she shouted. "You are my godmother, you *have* to save me! When will you come?"

For the rest of the day she sat by the barbed wire fence, staring into the distance, refusing to eat, waiting for Dada and Anna Maria. Messelo knelt beside her, his head on her shoulder.

"Dada will burst through the outer fence in a truck," Settela mumbled, her voice hoarse from crying. "We must be ready to jump in the back of his lorry before the guards start shooting at us. Then we'll all drive back to Holland and live in our old caravan near Anna Maria's house. In the place where I was born. We'll wash ourselves in Anna Maria's bathroom and she'll teach us to read."

She pointed at a glint of silver in the twilight sky. "Look, Messelo, the magic star! Let's shut our eyes and make a wish. If we wish hard enough, the lorries will come and rescue us!"

"Rescue us," Messelo chuckled. Settela looked at her little brother. His head was rough with black thorny stubble. His eyes, once so bright, had sunk into his sallow face. His cheeks were hollow. He looked like an old man.

I wonder what I look like, Settela thought, running her fingers through her short greasy hair. People used to say I was pretty. But back then, when I was young, I had long hair and clean skin.

Cradling Messelo in her arms, she gazed at the stars twinkling in the purple dusk, waiting for Dada and Anna Maria to drive up. And then she heard the sound of approaching trucks.

"Our wish has come true!" she laughed, jumping up and hugging Messelo. "They're coming to free us from this stinking dump! From the dirty smoke and lousy beds."

Triumphantly, she rushed back into the barrack with her news. "Listen, Mammie, the lorries are coming at last! Dada's coming! We're going home!"

Startled, Mam picked up Doosje, while Aunt Buta placed a protective hand on Tikono's shoulder. The lorries came nearer and nearer, screeching to a halt nearby. There was banging and shouting. Rough commands. Wailing in the neighbouring block.

Settela glanced at Mam in surprise. She'd expected to hear laughter and singing, not the sound of frightened voices.

"Climb on my shoulders, Settela!" ordered Aunt Buta. "Look out of the window—tell us what's going on."

She bent down and Settela wriggled onto her aunt's bony back, hauling herself up.

She gasped. She clawed at the wall to steady herself.

Outside, herded from the barrack opposite, old men, women and children were being pushed onto lorries. Anyone who tried to run away was beaten back by guards.

When the lorries were full, the prisoners were driven off.

Young Dina and Fremdi were squashed into one of the trucks. Looking round frantically, they saw Settela at the window. Imploringly they stretched out their hands. Then they were gone.

When Settela was lowered to the ground, she couldn't speak. She pressed her hands to her chest to stop the pain.

At last she gulped, "It wasn't Anna Maria! She hasn't come."

"What are you saying, girl?" Mam asked sharply. "What did you see?"

"They put them in a lorry! The guards hit them if they were too slow! Mammie, we must run away now, before it's too late!"

Mam looked small and shrunken. "No child! They won't come for us. If we run, we'll be shot. We'll be alright. Your father will be here soon."

Smiling, Mam sat on the bed with Doosje in her arms. Settela, Sonja and Messelo nestled close to her.

"Listen," Mam murmured. "Can you hear him playing?"

Settela listened.

The barrack was filled with the haunting notes of a violin. Dada was playing her favourite tune.

Chapter 19

Settela started to hum to Dada's melody. The humming grew louder, filling the barrack with sweet music.

The noise turned into the throbbing of engines. The lorries were returning to the compound.

Settela held her breath, willing them to go away. She wanted to stay in the barrack. She prayed that the door wouldn't open.

There was a thunderous crack and the door swung crazily on its hinges, squeaking like a dying pig. Huge guards rushed into the long room, pulling everyone up.

"On your feet! *Alles raus! Schnell!* Take your things. You're being sent on a journey!"

Mam grabbed Doosje and Messelo. Settela stuffed clothes and scraps of food into the sack.

There was a sharp smell in the air. It came from the prisoners and Settela frowned, trying to remember where she'd smelt it before.

When a soldier lifted her into the lorry, she kicked her legs violently, trying to wriggle away from his hard fingers. "No use struggling, little Gypsy," he told her, jamming her down between Sonja and Mam.

Settela squeezed to the side of the lorry and looked out.

"Are we off to the land of candyfloss now?" Messelo asked her.

"Yes," she nodded.

With an angry roar, the lorry revved up and jolted down the track, passing thin ragged starpeople plodding back from the fields. Settela wanted to wave to them, but they didn't look up.

She sniffed. "Now I recognise the smell, Mammie. It's the same smell that comes from Farmer Bruin's cows when they're sent to be slaughtered."

When her mother smiled, the lines on her face disappeared and her eyes shone. "That's right, my sweet. We're going to work on a farm. With Kali and Blieta. Your father'll be there as well, and Willy and Elmo. Uncle Koleman and Uncle Rico too. We'll work in the fresh air. We'll eat eggs. We'll milk cows and pick fruit, just like we do each summer."

Settela remembered. There had been another life. Last year when she was eight, moving from farm to farm during harvest. There'd been fields for the caravan, hay for the horse, twigs for the fire, fresh water, eggs sizzling in yellow butter, mopped up with soft bread.

Ashy smuts settled on the blue marks on her arm and she coughed, wiping away the dirt with her ragged skirt. "We're slowing down!" yelled Django, then he leaned across and put his mouth to Settela's ear. "This may be your last chance, dear child!" he told her. "You're young, you can make it. As soon as we stop, grab Messelo and Sonja, and run as fast as you can. You must get away!"

Settela nodded, her heart thumping as she remembered Yosef, the Jewish man shot on the tracks back in Holland.

The lorry braked outside the chimney building, and a waiting soldier ran over to lower the tailpiece. *"Machen schnell!"* he commanded, but his voice was low and gentle. He helped Mam down, and lifted Sonja carefully onto the ground.

"Why's he crying!" asked Settela in surprise. Mam was looking round, searching for something.

A shudder ran down Settela's neck. Mam's looking for somewhere to hide, she thought. She wants to escape. She knows something awful's going to happen.

Smoke merged into the evening shadows, making it impossible to see clearly. There were so many prisoners pressed together, so many guards. "We *will* get away, but we must wait for the right moment," Settela mumbled.

Aunt Buta was pressing her hands to her head, twisting the ends of her scarf in her fingers.

Whispers were flying round.

"They're going to delouse us."

"They're going to shave our heads again."

"We're going to have a bath."

"A bath," Settela murmured. "Clean water. Wash away the filth. Drown the lice."

"We were so clean before," Mam was saying to Old Maira. "So strong. Now my little one can hardly move!" She kissed Doosje's face.

Maira snorted. "It's those cursed Nazis who've made us dirty! May the lice gnaw their damned corpses forever!"

Settela wondered what was going to happen next. Although the guards had told them they were going on a journey, she couldn't see any railway lines, and the building in front of her didn't look like a station. Aunt Buta said it must be the washhouse.

The lorries drove off, leaving the group of Sintis in the moonlight.

Something very strange is going on, Settela thought. She stood as close as she could to Mam, clutching her mother's skirt.

"Where are the Gypsies from the other block, Mammie? Where are Dina and Fremdi?"

She looked round for her friends. Maybe they'd run to the woods and were sitting round a fire, eating berries and drinking goat's milk sweetened with wild honey. Making plans to rescue the Gypsies left behind in the camp.

At first the sound was faint, like a distant hammer beating nails into wood. As the noise came closer, she realised it was the thud of boots stamping along the gravel path. Settela stiffened, gripping Messelo's shoulder as armed soldiers marched up to the group of waiting prisoners.

Aunt Buta let out a shrill wail as a big black car, driven by a uniformed chauffeur, came into sight. A beautiful woman in a red lace dress sat in the back seat, smiling out of the window.

Laughing, shouting with relief, Settela waved and pointed as the car drew up.

Her voice rang out. "It's her! At last! Anna Maria! In her black car!" She grinned as everyone turned to stare at her. For the first time in her life, people were listening to what she had to say.

"I told you she'd come. My godmother, Anna Maria Duysens! My Dutch name's Anna Maria, you know. I was named after her. She held me when I was baptised, even though Father Jacobs doesn't like Gypsies. Beggars and riffraff, he calls us. But Anna Maria, the doctor's wife, she likes Gypsies. She's come to save us!"

The dream had come true, just like she'd always known it would. Beaming, she spoke to her mother, to her starving brothers and sisters. "Just follow me! I'm going to rescue you! Me and Anna Maria, we'll take you home!"

Mam gasped in shock. "Stop your gabbling, girl, before you get yourself shot! Have you gone mad? That's not Anna Maria! It's the Camp Commandant!"

Settela's voice died away. She shivered. She licked a flake of ash from her lip.

A man in an army jacket and cap got out of the car, his badges gleaming in the moonlight.

"No!" Settela wanted to shout. "This is wrong!" She stood silently, unable to believe her eyes.

The soldiers saluted as the Camp Commandant walked to the front of the crowd.

"Good evening," said the Commandant politely. "Please listen carefully."

The women looked at each other, muttering in low voices.

"You have nothing to worry about," the Commandant assured them. "You are going on a journey, so you must be clean. You will wash yourselves and your children, then put on new clothes."

New clothes. She was going to get a new dress. A red dress, with a frill round the hem, like the one Mam had made her for Doosje's baptism.

Maira twisted round, and Settela saw terror in the old woman's eyes. But Mam seemed calm and trusting.

Mam sighed. "When this is over, my dear children, we'll never eat dirty food again. We won't have lice. We'll grow our hair. We'll stay together forever, all our family."

She pulled Settela close. "Be brave, sweet child," she whispered. "Shine always like a star."

Mam embraced her children, whispering a blessing to each one.

Settela put her arms round Mam's waist. A feeling of peace washed over her. She hugged her brother and sisters, her aunt and cousins.

They stood together, clasping each other, waiting for the shower.

Chapter 20

She was in a shower room.

There were hoses round the walls.
There was the gushing of wind.
A sighing.
A stinging smell.
Tears streaming from eyes.
Howls coming from mouths.
Fingers scrabbling at walls.
There were arms holding her tight, hugging her, choking her.

There was a whiteness and a nothingness and a calmness and a silver cloud.
There was smoke drifting through the sky.
There was a sun shining in the heaven.
There were stars and a silver crescent moon.

There was a song that would never stop singing.

GLOSSARY

Sinti	the group name by which most Dutch Gypsies are known.	(Sinti dialect of Romani)
Sintiska	the language of the Sinti	"
Gadje	non-Gypsies.	
Mevrouw	madam	(Dutch)
Mijneer	mister	"
Raus	out	(German)
schnell	quick	"
gnädige Frau	madam	"
alles raus	everyone out	"
machen schnell	hurry up	"

HISTORICAL NOTES

1940 Holland occupied by German forces.

1943 Twenty-seven collection camps for all caravan dwellers set up.

May 16th 1944 Caravanners in collection camps rounded up, and sent to Kamp Westerbork.

May 19th 1944 Sinti group sent from Kamp Westerbork to Auschwitz.

July 31 1944 "Liquidation" of Gypsy camp in Auschwitz-Birchenau, often remembered as "Zigeunernacht".

It is estimated that well over a million and a half Romanies were slaughtered during World War II. Settela Steinbach was one of them.

AFTERWORD

The photograph of Settela Steinbach has inspired many people in many lands. Artists like Katarzyna Pollock have used her image in their work. Singers like the Dutch Robert Long have written songs about her.

So how did this little Sinti girl, one of countless thousands of Gypsies massacred because of Nazi racial policies, become an icon of the suffering of persecuted children in World War II?

In 1944, SS Obersturmführer Albert Konrad Gemmeker, the German commander of Kamp Westerbork, ordered Jewish prisoner Rudolf Breslauer to record life in the Dutch transit camp, including the Tuesday transports which took inmates away to their fate. On one such Tuesday, Rudolf Breslauer filmed a train leaving Kamp Westerbork for Auschwitz.

A little Sinti girl was looking out of the cattle wagon as Breslauer filmed. Her name was Settela Steinbach. She was 9 years old. She was murdered in Auschwitz a few months later.

Although her haunting picture became world famous after the war, it wasn't until some fifty years after her death that Dutch journalist Aad Wagenaar discovered the identity of "the girl in the wagon door." In 1995, his account of his long search to find out the name of the unknown child was published in Holland by *Arbeiderspers*. He called his book SETTELA.

SETTELA'S LAST ROAD was inspired by Breslauer's famous photograph, and by Aad Wagenaar's book. SETTELA'S LAST ROAD is an imaginative interpretation of the facts provided by Aad Wagenaar's painstaking work.

Aad Wagenaar's book has been reissued in Dutch by *Just Publishers b.v.,* together with a DVD of Breslauer's film.
www.justpublishers.nl
SETTELA, Aad Wagenaar's factual account, is available in English from Five Leaves Publications, www.fiveleaves.com